*Her prose reveals an intimacy with the South that can't be faked, and this authenticity is part of what enables her to move so fluidly between gorgeous sensory images and scenes of horrifying emotional power. Also, it's always nice when a crime writer actually understands police work. . . . Susan Anderson is a natural storyteller.*

**- Michael Carr -** Editor or copyeditor of over 300 books, including Brad Meltzer's political thriller *The Zero Game*; Archer Mayor's *Chat, Gatekeeper*, and *The Second Mouse*; and several of Donald Westlake's Dortmunder books.

*Susan Anderson's carefully crafted tale of an unsolved murder in an old-fashioned town with old-fashioned secrets is as nostalgic as it is ominous. Personally, I wouldn't be caught dead in the town of Ellyson. Then again, maybe I would...*

**- Taylor Mali -** one of the original poets to appear on the HBO original series *Russell Simmons Presents Def Poetry*. He received a New York Foundation for the Arts Grant in 2001 to develop *Teacher! Teacher!* a one-man show about poetry, teaching, and math which won the jury prize for best solo performance at the 2001 U. S. Comedy Arts Festival. He has narrated several books on tape, including *The Great Fire* for which he won the Golden Earphones Award for children's narration.

*To Ruthie,*

*Fondly,*

*Sus Anderson*

# Cold Case
# in
# Ellyson

Susan Anderson

You know also that the beginning is the most important
part of any work, especially in the case of a young and
tender thing;
for that is the time at which the character is being formed
and the desired impression is more readily taken.

Plato

*My grandfather, the sheriff; my grandmother, the teacher; my
evening shift partner, John, the inspiration; my mother, Kay,
the spy-wanna-be; my father, Arden, the cheerleader; my aunt
Catherine, the rock; my sister, Duchess, the keeper of memories;
my husband, Jim, the genius; and my sons, Cole and Connor,
the reason. I am grateful to you all.*

# PART I

## CHAPTER I

I can't decide just how much the town has changed over the years. The backdrop of buildings looks and feels familiar, but I am aware that certain details have altered the complexion of the area. For example, I clearly remember many of the buildings on Main Street, but most now stand vacant and in disrepair. The five-and-dime is still open, and the hardware store next to it seems little changed. The same two churches still flank the square, one I particularly remember well ablaze with a fresh coat of white paint. A telltale spattered ladder still leans against the entrance; only the steeple remains untouched. It seems to me that they should have started at the top and worked their way down, but then again, I've never painted a church. Across the well-kept square, punctuated with its beds of geraniums blooming between marble benches and the once bubbling pool, the other church squats on weathered haunches, as if to hide its chipping paint and exposed splinters from the stare of its cousin. Beyond the square, the Rex Movie Theater marquee touts some coming attraction, no doubt long since come and gone. All that remains of its name are a few random vowels and nonsensical consonants, signifying nothing.

My next–to-last trip to Ellyson was the last time I saw my grandmother alive, and back then I took little notice of this town, too young to consider it of any importance. I was not behind the wheel, but rather stretched out in the backseat of my parents' station wagon, admiring my newly acquired white patent leather shoes. The most riveting thing about those shoes was neither their shine nor their style. It was their heels, the slight elevation that symbolized my first step beyond childhood, and I was enchanted with how my dainty feet filled them. As Florida fell away and Alabama approached, I grew more and more excited about sharing them with my grandmother.

Downtown Ellyson—and I use the term loosely—dissolved into the hickory- and catalpa-shaded streets of my grandmother's neighborhood without my notice, but when the car turned into her unpaved driveway, I rose up knowing I was there and skipped from the car into that fine, red clay that, within seconds, had dusted the hem of my frilly white dress and the bottoms of my new white shoes. Near the front of the house, an old banty rooster nosed about for a nibble of something in the hollyhocks. I called him Charlie, Charlie the Chicken, and he usually ignored me, as he did this day. The front door to the white clapboard house stood wide open, the screen door unlocked, as it always was.

"Why, Katy, I think you've grown an inch since I last saw you! Come here, honey, and give Grandma a hug." She always called me Katy, never Kathleen. I felt the familiar softness of her hug and smelled the bacon grease on her spattered green apron.

"Grandma, I have *not* grown a bit. It's my new shoes, see?" I pointed to my new shoes (now a little dusty) with a one-inch heel.

"Sarah, you're putting heels on a seven-year-old?" She suddenly realized I had let go of her hand, ashamed to have on those silly shoes. "Oh, honey," she said, "they're fine, really. You're just growing up way too fast." Temporarily mollified, I punctuated her quick recovery with a twirl.

Now, nearly two decades later, a swirl of red earth covers my windshield as I approach that same dirt driveway. The sudden wash of familiarity is quickly trumped by a feeling of uneasiness. Years of inattention have left the house dilapidated. Black shutters that I don't remember at all have fallen into what were once flowerbeds or else hang by a single rusty hinge. I wonder why no one has complained about the height of the careless weeds and the condition of the property, until I note that all the other neighborhood homes are in equally abhorrent condition. The driveway runs down the left side of the house, and this is where I park. I grab the key I took from my parents' house, not really believing I'll need it, and approach the threshold. This time, I'm wearing tennis shoes.

I am surprised to find the heavy wooden door locked. None of the windows are broken either, and it looks as though the house has only been ignored, not mistreated. The key slips in easily, and I turn the lock. As I enter, a fine fog of dust kicks up around me. The living room, now bare of all furniture and rugs, seems so much smaller than it does in my memory, but I consider that childhood often distorts reality. To the left of the entryway stands the doorway to my grandfather's bedroom. Injured in a car crash before I was born, his back tormented him to the point that, according to Grandma, he left the marital bed to give her an uninterrupted night's sleep. I can picture his double bed made of honey oak, and the simple pine table that served as his nightstand. Once it held a hurricane lamp and a pile of books from which he read during the bouts of pain that woke him in the night. I remember Hemingway was among his favorite authors—probably why Hemingway is also one of mine. My grandfather's misery ended in a farm accident less than two years before my grandmother's murder. He was working on some of his acreage during his day off as sheriff of Whitcomb County—not that he ever *really* had a day off. Grandpa was such a big, muscular man, it seemed as though nothing could harm him, but somehow he fell off his own tractor, and it kept right on moving, crushing him under the rear wheel before it finally hung up in the wire fence and stalled. We happened to be at their house the day I first heard those wails of loss. Grandpa was late joining us for lunch, and Grandma sent a neighborhood boy to fetch him from the field. The boy didn't come back, but his parents did. All I remember hearing were screams and the screen door slamming once and then again. His was my first funeral, and I remember little of it. I'm sorry he never knew that I followed in his vocational footsteps. I'm even sorrier that Grandma never knew.

Grandpa's room connects to a bathroom that in turn opens into Grandma's bedroom. Within that narrow space, I notice that the claw-foot tub's enamel is chipped in places and rusting. The lace shower curtain that Grandma made is absent. All that remains is the rod that Grandpa fashioned from a galvanized steel pipe. I am not ready to open the next door.

Back in the living room, I proceed into the small third bedroom that Grandma used as her sewing room. Many times, while she held me in her lap, she would let me press the wrought-iron treadle of her old Singer with the tips of my shoes, heelless shoes, which could just reach it. Her deft fingers could readily make a hem or buttonhole or anything else she chose. I inherited none of her homemaking skills, perhaps because my mother never did. It seems to me that Grandma was always creating while my mother was always busy trying to recreate that which already was. Grandma gave life, and Mom tried to readjust it; she still does. If she knew I was here today, for instance, she would consider it an affront to her delicate familial sensibilities. It could get too messy, open up memories better left buried away. Admittedly, I never fully understood the working model of the matriarchal relationships in my family until I matured into adulthood, which really didn't occur until I was in my early twenties. When I was a child, my mother served as a barometer of what was acceptable and what was not. I think that is still true even today. Grandma was different. She accepted me; mother directed me. I think Mother tried to direct Grandma, too, and in some strange way that I do not yet understand, their strained relationship became mine. I've never been able to pin down a reason why my mother was so different from her own, but I have often wondered if Mother was ashamed of her small-town beginnings. She did all she could to direct me toward a life less humble than that of her own family. She wanted me to find greatness, and she didn't believe that could happen in a small town. And the fact is, I've realized her greatest fears. It's a fact I cannot forget.

What I remember as I walk into Grandma's kitchen today is that here, there was nothing but joy, hers and mine. I can still remember how as a child I stood transfixed, watching the sugary glaze as it sank into the still-warm lemon cake, perfectly formed, as all of Grandma's Bundt cakes were. She was a quiet woman except when it came to her laughter. Not that she was loud, but her soft giggles permeated every nook of her old house just as that thick, sweet icing seeped into that cake. Although I know she must have had other dresses, the only one I distinctly recall is a red, flowery one, with cloth-covered buttons dotting all the way up the front. The dress covered most of her broad body except for her fleshy, freckled pale arms, which jiggled with every motion, and her sturdy calves, which were often hidden behind heavy hosiery. Her feet and shoes I can't picture at all—it is as though she floated from cabinet to counter to table. Emma Johnson, the dowdy but loving widow of Otis, lifetime resident of Ellyson, Alabama: mother, grandmother, homemaker—all of which is a good deal more than anyone could say of me. Single and childless, I grew from a dainty little girl into the body of a teenage boy with the heart of a woman. Today in high heels, I no doubt look as ridiculous as I did to Grandma's eye when I was seven.

Without forethought, using the hem of my T-shirt, I begin to wipe away coats of dust and grease from the old enameled white gas stove and oven. The ice box, its door ajar, offers a variety of dead bugs that found their resting place there, and I am not concerned with disturbing their peace. Pale yellow Formica countertops, once speckled with gold, have faded almost to white. The unfinished pine cupboards are now tacky with a coating of dust and humidity deposited by years of neglect.

As I look into what was once the dining area, I remember Grandma telling me how to set a lady's table using the good silver and fine china she kept buried away in the buffet. I don't know what she used on other days, but every time we ate at Grandma's, I was told to retrieve her breakables from their hiding place. Few of the plates matched each other in design, but they were all flowery and delicate and astonishingly thin, and I picked them up cautiously and transferred them, one at a time, onto the table. All the glasses were colored a dusty rose and etched with ivy. The silverware was heavy and polished to a brilliant luster, although utterly void of artistic detail. "It's all ready, Grandma," I'd call into the kitchen, and she would complete the final embellishment: a centerpiece of forget-me-nots, arranged in a shallow silver bowl.

Standing here in the dust and silence, I can almost smell the aroma of biscuits and chicken that always seemed to emanate from her kitchen. Grandma would draw out a heavy cast-iron skillet with both hands and bang it noisily down on the stove. Her head would briefly disappear as she pulled out a tray from the ice box, with the chicken parts already floured for frying. "Stay back," she would warn as she dropped them, spitting and popping, into the grease. Today that hissing sound reminds me of many of the conversations, mostly arguments, that passed between the women of our family, with Mom always as the common denominator. Grandma and I never fought. But maybe that's not fair, since Grandma and I never had the chance.

My attention is suddenly drawn back to the present by a dog barking outside the back of the house. From the kitchen, I unlatch the door that leads to the mud room, the small room where deliveries of groceries and milk were deposited so many years ago. The door that leads from it to the back porch always stayed unlocked, as it is now—just as my grandmother would have left it.

"Did I tell you about the time your grandfather went to meet a killer at the train station?" Grandma once asked me in a mysterious tone. We were sitting inside the screened-in porch out back where Grandma would rock in her olive-green-painted wicker chair as she shelled peas, deftly running a thumb down the pods. She let me think I was helping her, but my fingers were never as dexterous.

"No, Grandma, you never told me that one," I'd always say, even if the story sounded familiar.

"Well, not long after Otis became sheriff, he got word that a killer from Tallahassee would be riding the train to Ellyson to visit some of his kinfolk just outside of town. Grandpa told me he would meet the train, but when the time came to go, he walked out of the house without his revolver.

"'Otis, what about your gun?' I called to him.

"'Oh, won't need it. He ain't gonna cause me no trouble. Guns just make things messy,' he answered back, and smiled just a little. I didn't let on how scared I was for him. He came back home about three hours later, and I can't tell you how relieved I was.

"'Did you get him?' I asked.

"'Of course. Didn't have a lick of trouble.'

"'He didn't even put up a fight?' I had trouble believing him.

"'No, he came along peaceably.'

"He never carried a gun, Katy—said there was no need for it. And I have to say, he never did need it. No man ever touched or ran from your Grandpa. They respected him and his badge. Grandpa used to say, 'If you roll around in dirt, you're going to get dirty.' He worked in a difficult world, Kathleen, but he never let himself become a piece of it."

She didn't know it, but Grandpa was my hero. I can picture him: tall and big, with hands that seem too large even for his oversized frame—a man a little slow to smile. Neither of my grandparents would understand the world in which I work, the hits I've taken, the number of times I've drawn my gun. No doubt Grandpa would be disappointed to know that the badge doesn't mean that much anymore, that it so rarely instills respect these days.

One of my most vivid memories is of Grandpa letting me steer his tractor around the property. One of his hands always rested on top of the throttle, just in case. We would skirt the woods behind the houses sometimes, and he would point out by name all the trees and plants we came across. Grandpa seemed more comfortable with facts than feelings. I don't remember him telling me he loved me, but I know that he did. And I don't remember knowing him, the kind of man he was, but I do know I loved him.

Forcing myself to unwrap from these memories, I drift back to the here and now and notice telltale signs of unauthorized entry onto the porch. Grandma never much believed in the value of having a pet, so she would be a little disheartened to see that a cat has found a surrogate home here. The screens that once covered the three sides of the porch are gone, and an old gray towel nestled in the corner is coated with fine blond hairs. Beyond this porch lies the dirt road alleyway that admits access to the back of all the neighborhood yards, although it is clear that no one has maintained the property around here for many years. No new developments have invaded the woods behind the drive, and the land seems forsaken.

During that last visit to Grandma's—a time I've never allowed myself to forget, not even the slightest detail—I walked through the mudroom and onto the back porch to look for a neighbor's playful dog that often wandered behind the house. But a pinpoint of light deep in the woods caught my eye, and I noticed a man walking among the trees with something over his shoulder, perhaps an ax or a scythe. In a moment, he disappeared into the dense brush. I opened the screen door trying to catch another glimpse and noticed it was sprinkling so lightly that it was difficult to see the individual misty droplets. Grandma called me back. "Katy, dinner's almost ready, and you need to wash up, you hear?" I can still hear her slight southern drawl— something else I didn't acquire, although I wouldn't have minded it.

I shut the back door and return to the interior of the house. The kitchen opens into the dining room, today just an empty space that bleeds back into the living room. I don't recall many conversations that passed over Grandma's worn and stained oak table, but I do recall that last one, and I do remember Grandma giggling, the way her cheeks rose toward her radiant blue eyes when she laughed. My focus always seemed to rest on her soft, wavy white hair, parted girlishly low on the left side, cut short and combed smooth. Grandma put all the food on the table and sat down to stir the sugar in her freshly steeped mint tea. "Sarah, I think I'm ready to sell the house and farm and move to be closer to you all," she said as she looked directly at me.

Mother's chewing stopped abruptly. "Well, I'm sure it would mean a lot to Kathleen." I couldn't contain myself. I jumped down from my cane chair, ran to Grandma and planted a wet kiss on her cheek. She giggled behind her napkin.

"Now, Katy, go sit down now and eat your supper. You'll have plenty of time for that later." One look at Grandma's face and I knew she wasn't mad, but I sat down anyway, replaced my napkin on my lap, took a big bite of chicken and smiled open-mouthed at her.

"Close your mouth right now, young lady," Mother admonished, and I knew she was displeased with my poor manners, the child too often heard, too often seen, who never quite learned how not to express herself, even when it was in her best interest.

Hoping that my mom and dad, embroiled in some deep discussion, would not notice my disappearance or care if they did, I walked across Grandma's hardwood floors, which pleasantly accentuated the click-clack of my heels on the floor. I strolled over to the sideboard with its primitively etched front and scratched surface and picked up a heavy silver picture frame, immune from tarnish and dust. It was a black-and-white picture of a man. Humble-looking yet imposing, he stood tall against the frame house, holding a dark brimmed hat in his hands, clearly uncomfortable, clearly posing for a picture. Other than in this photograph, I never saw my grandpa look ill-at-ease. Perhaps he knew what would happen that night. My parents stayed seated at the table, stirred their tea, and spoke in hushed tones. I was familiar with this "not-in-front-of-the-child" routine, but that doesn't mean I didn't listen.

Mother spoke to Grandma in a whisper I wasn't meant to hear: "Mom, we got a letter last week from Gracie. She's insisting that she has the deed to Carson Acres. We need to figure this out before you get rid of your house." Gracie Jackson was Grandpa's only living sibling. Grandma had seldom said a kind word about her, and I had never met her. "She said Dad deeded his half of the land to her a few months before his death." I had visited Carson Acres a few times, but only once since

Grandpa died. That's where we would go fishing with our cane poles and the bucket of worms we dug up in the backyard. The oversized pond was hidden in dense woods, a good distance from the end of the dirt road. Grandpa and I would walk, usually in silence, to a rock outcropping that jutted out over the bank. In the peace of it all, Grandpa would tell me, in a low voice, tales of his adventures as a boy growing up in the backwoods of Alabama. One I distinctly recall was about the time he jumped into a moving train car outside Montgomery. He had thought the car was empty, but instead he landed in a car full of transients—"hobos" he called them—who tried to steal the boots off his feet. That was the day, he said, he decided to become a lawman.

"Gracie was a fool the day she was born," Grandma replied as she wiped the spilled tea from her chin. "They inherited that land in 'forty-two, and Gracie knows it became half mine when Otis died. I'd like to see the paper that says different."

"She claims to have something in writing, Mom, and she said you've seen it," my mother responded a little hesitantly.

"Oh, yes, I've seen her hen-scratching, and if she tries to claim that Otis's hand wrote that, she's more a fool than Crazy Harry," the harmless derelict who rarely put two coherent sentences together and was the local drunk.

Even with my back turned, I could tell that my mother was upset, not because she was yelling, but because she spoke in whispers. Grandma fell silent. Grandma is still silent.

I have not been in Grandma's room since the day of her funeral, and I am hesitant to pass over that threshold. Rather than mellowed by age, my memories seem more alive, more graphic than ever, yet I know I must force myself inside. I pass through the doorway tentatively and am taken aback by the stark whiteness of her room. Unlike Grandpa's room and the living room, her room at first appears free of the grime of untouched years and neglect—spotless and sanitary as a hospital room. But as I draw closer to the windows and walls, my eyes adjust to the dimming light, and a pall seems to cover the room. A faint contrast against the wood floor marks the outline of her bed, the site of her final breath. I force myself to imagine the scene of her murder, but my mind's images seem to distort as I feel a sudden film of cold sweat suddenly release from my pores. I want to leave. I want to be able to breathe. I struggle to open some windows for circulation. Using my pocket knife, I am finally able to jimmy two of the three sashes open. But even the fresh air I breathe in seems to have too little oxygen, and I rush out the front door to my car, inhale a few deep breaths, and grab my flashlight. My professional self seems to take over.

I go back inside now, looking for something — anything—that can tell me more about what happened in this house. Now, just over seventeen years after the fact, it seems a ridiculous hope, but I am drawn inside. I return to her bedroom and, holding the beam of my flashlight against the walls, search for some telling mark, some reason she might have been killed. I find nothing. I check her bedroom for any clues, scratch marks, anything, but still nothing. Distraught, I wander back to the comfortable room, the kitchen, with its warmth and memories.

Soon after my parents and I drove away after our last Sunday dinner together with Grandma, she was murdered in her bed. My parents wouldn't tell me the details (Mother always believed in shielding me, especially from the truth), but a few years later, while snooping in my mother's closet, I found some newspaper clippings.

The *Ellyson Gazette* described it in this way: "Dearly loved Emma Johnson, widow of Sheriff Otis Johnson, was brutally murdered in her home on Escambia Drive last night. Sheriff McAllister says it's the worst killing he's ever seen. 'There was blood everywhere, and we can't find one thing missing. Killed for nothing.'" The article went on to say that it was the first murder in the county in four years. I was at school when my mother got the news. Corry, our housekeeper, picked me up early from the school lunchroom and told me Grandma had died. Until today, I hadn't been able to remember, or maybe just didn't want to remember, any more of that day.

My second funeral was worse, probably because I was older and closer to Grandma, and probably, too, because Mom, lost in her own misery, was incapable of consoling me. She could barely care for herself. I can remember my father having to tell her to get dressed for the funeral and telling her what to wear. Mother was so numb, she had difficulty getting off the couch. My poor dad did the best he could to keep us going. The casket remained closed, and the funeral was held in Ellyson at the small country Baptist church, the one I noticed today, recently painted. As we walked out following the casket, I noticed that not only the church was full but also the driveway and parking lot, too, just full of people. I couldn't imagine there were that many people in the whole town. The cemetery was a couple of miles away from the church, and we marched in the bright sunlight toward the darkest hole I had ever seen. It seemed like hours before we could get away from there. Someone handed me a daisy from the arrangement on the casket; I still have the brown stem. The petals have all been lost.

We drove back to Grandma's house. A lot of cars were already there, but they left a space for us in front. I was afraid to go in, but Daddy told me no bad men would be there. "I'm not scared of *them*, Daddy," I assured him. I walked in hesitantly but then darted from room to room, looking for something. My answer came in the absences. Her bedroom was all wrong: no white coverlet, no crisply pressed sheets, no pillows, no mattress, no hand-woven throw rug on the floor. The room smelled of bleach and ammonia. No one had to tell me where Grandma had been killed. I ran to the hall bathroom and threw up.

As I washed my face and noticed my reflection in the mirror above it, an image caught my eye. Sometimes after our family dinners, Grandma and I would work on our cross-stitching projects. I was working on a Raggedy Ann, and she was finishing her sampler the last time I saw her. It was now hanging on the bathroom wall, which meant she must have hung it the night she was killed. Ironically, it said, "Judge not, and ye shall not be judged: condemn not, and ye shall not be condemned; forgive, and ye shall be forgiven." She told me that this was the only way to live. I believed that, for a while. The words reverberated in my mind. Some of us were good, and some of us were bad. I could see no blank space in between. I still can't, and I believe it's something I learned at seven, when the warmest part of my life melted away into a casket in a backwoods cemetery. Maybe that's the attraction of working as a cop. I am not there to judge; the laws are clearly written, and my only charge is to enforce them. Motives are for lawyers, judgments for juries. I choose to have little part in either. I never saw more clearly the line that separates truth from fiction than in my line of work. The lines are so distinct in crime, the quantities so well known, that there is little need to interpret or question the laws. One night we were called to a disturbance, and as we neared the steps to the front porch, a man appeared, poised with a two-by-four held directly over my partner's head. He threatened, and so did we—with Glocks. He crossed the line, and we offered him a choice: drop his weapon or we would drop him—all perfectly legal and acceptable. He made the wiser choice, and we responded by making the legal one. It's like someone blowing through a red light: the colors are very clear.

What seems like an hour has somehow grown closer to three, so I decide to pack it in and try to find the local sheriff's office. Before I leave, I feel as though I need to tell Grandma goodbye in some way, so I return to her room, to the place where her bed was, to the side of the bed where she slept. As I approach that place, I notice that one floorboard is not flush with the others. A slit of light passing in between two tree branches reflects against the raised board, making it more pronounced from the others, as if out of place. I step on it and feel the floor buckle slightly beneath my foot. My flashlight illuminates small gaps on either side of the wooden plank. I pull out my pocket knife and try to pry it loose, and I am taken aback by how readily it gives way. Placing the floorboard aside, I shine my flashlight into the crevice, fearful of what I might find. The beam lights up a flour sack that appears partially full and next to it a swatch of cloth tied with heavy cord around some object. I lift both discoveries out and am suddenly terrified, as though I have unlocked some supernaturally guarded tomb, releasing the demons of evil that are now hovering around me. Had the room not been empty and the light been just right, I probably never would have noticed anything telltale in the floor, and I sense that Grandma planned it just this way, that she made me return to this room at just the moment I would notice what had never been noticed before. Snatching the two items, I replace the board and heed the urge to leave the house. And oddly, more than anything else, I want my mother. I want to sit across from her at her immaculate kitchen table, pristine mostly from lack of use, and hear her tell me that my hair's too long or my face too pale, as if these were the biggest problems in the world. But I have never been able to go to my mother when I needed her most. I slam each window shut, and still clutching the newly found treasures and my flashlight, I walk out wondering what happened to Raggedy Ann.

## CHAPTER II

There was a time when I was very good at walking out, certainly on friends or boyfriends, but absolutely on family. I seem to have this internal light switch that, once thrown, takes rewiring to undo. Like the time my ex-boyfriend got angry with me in public in New Orleans. The driver, for some unknown reason, had told all the passengers to get off and wait for the next trolley. Alan made some snide comment about it to the driver, and I, not really wanting a scene, told Alan to forget about it. Well, he couldn't, and then he yelled at me. Blink. In an instant, it went from day to night in my mind, and that was the last date I had with Alan. Another heretofore unknown, unforgivable sin. I guess that's why I'm not married. I have too many lines, and too many people accidentally cross them. It's sometimes worse with my mother. One of my latest power outages was with her. Mom invited me to join my parents and some of their old friends who were coming to town for a brief visit. I adore the Joneses and agreed to come along. That is, until another evening-shift officer asked me to trade a day off because he had to leave unexpectedly for some family crisis. Police officers have to work together, help each other out. It was important for him to go, so I agreed. Mother was irate.

"I specifically told the Joneses you would be there. They will be very disappointed. And I'm disappointed in you for making our plans less important than some cop's," she spat over the phone when I told her.

"That *cop* is my friend, my backup, and he needs a favor, and I'm going to help him out. I'm sorry that interferes with your plans, I really am, but it just does." I usually try to be a little more respectful.

"I don't know what's worse," Mom said, "you being a cop or that damned better-than-you attitude." She hesitated for a moment. "I think it's you being a cop."

I slammed the phone down, turned the lock on that emotional door. A younger Kathleen might have waited a week to accept Mom's calls or knocks, but I answered her call the very next day. She's not going to change, nor will I. We're more alike than I care to admit.

But I hope that what I found here in Ellyson will help her in some way. I unlock the door of my car and sit down, breathless. I haven't mustered up the nerve to look at what Grandma must have hidden, buried away for so many years. I am both intrigued and terrified. But I have to know. The sack is loosely tied at the top with braided cord. I hold my breath as I unwind it. I peel the skin of the sack and see that Grandma had hidden money, lots of money. There are stacks of bills, apparently all twenties, once bound in bunches with rubber bands, all of which have broken or rotted from age. I was never privy to Grandma's financial situation or even knew if she had a bank account, but in any event, she had entrusted perhaps a few thousand dollars to the innards of her home—money she wasn't comfortable putting anywhere else.

I turn to the other treasure. Wrapped within the cloth is a book, a leather-bound diary of sorts. The unlined pages contain a journal of some kind, with its first entry in 1941.

*December 19th, 1941*
*It seems fitting that I begin this diary on the*
*day I begin my new life with Otis. At 3:00*
*today we'll be married. I'm not really scared*
*because he's a good man.*

Maybe that should be my litmus test for marriage: a man who doesn't scare me. Not that I'm really frightened of men—I've dated several, but I've always found myself rather indifferent to them, except for the ones I work with, anyway. Not that I have a romantic attachment to anyone on the job, but they're a part of my family, and I love them with that familial part of my soul. We are there for one another both on and off duty.

The entries are sporadically penned in, with some years skipped altogether. It seems only the milestones merited a place within these pages, mostly births, marriages and deaths, with a few exceptions. One omission I do note strikes me as unbelievably odd. There is no mention of the birth of her own child, my mother, anywhere within the pages. I pull back on the binding to see if perhaps a page has been torn out, and am relieved to find a lingering fringe. The only reason that makes any sense is that my mother's birth and first months of life were a little shaky. Mom aspirated some fluid during labor, and the doctors weren't sure she would make it. Perhaps on that missing page my grandmother wrote of a doom that never came to pass.

Mom's marriage is clearly mentioned, however.

*July 31, 1973*
*Sarah's wedding day. I do declare, I have*
*mixed feelings. I think Andrew will be a*

*good husband to her, but I'm a little
concerned about the kind of wife she will
make.*

I can't believe Grandma actually felt that way
about her own daughter. I wonder if she ever told Mom
how she felt.

> *March 17, 1977*
> *My first grandchild was born today. We're
> going to drive up in the morning to see
> her, Kathleen. Sarah says she's healthy as a
> horse, and I heard her lungs – plenty
> healthy, all right. I'm so thankful. Lord
> help them both. She has a head full of dark
> hair and blue eyes. I'm going to spoil her
> rotten.*

She didn't really have a chance to do the damage
she proposed. I can't complain too much about my
childhood, or even my adulthood, but I have not been
spoiled. I had to earn all I got. I still do. I no longer feel I
have the unconditional love that parents are said to have
for their children, as if there's some cutoff date, some
"Use before…" stamp. They, especially Mom, look at me
now as an adult and judge me on the here and now, and
since they disapprove of the life I have chosen, I sense I
have lost their respect. And because it can't be earned
within my family, I must find it within myself.

I skip ahead to 1981, the year Grandpa died.

> *August 18, 1981*
> *August 16th marks the beginning of the
> end of my life. My sweetheart in high*

*school, the father of Sarah, my constant companion of nearly 40 years died in some fool accident. The Bells next door told me the news after I sent their son Jacob to hunt for Otis who was plowing the fields. Jacob found him a few feet away from the tractor, half buried in our crusty old land. It looked like the plow snagged a stump, knocked Otis off and ran him over. He was instantly crushed. It looks so ridiculous on paper even, a mountain of a man, a sheriff, dying in such an accident. I declare, I'll never fully believe it.*

Grandma never openly mourned Grandpa's death. When she spoke of him, it was always in a loving manner, but I suppose she must have come to terms with it when I wasn't around. After his funeral, I never saw a tear fall from her face.

*January 12, 1983*
*Gracie came over and offered me $25,000 for my half of Carson Acres. Seems like a good bit of money, but Otis told me to hang onto it if anything happened to him. He said it would be real valuable one day. I told her no, I didn't want to sell. She was plum fit to be tied.*

Gracie was the subject matter of my parents' conversation driving back from Ellyson that last night I saw my grandmother. I usually fell asleep on the drive home from Alabama, but that evening the discussion between my parents was too compelling for me to ignore.

"I can't understand Gracie. Why is that land so important to her? She has more acreage than Mom ever will."

"Maybe that's just it, dear. She just wants to make sure she's the biggest landowner in Ellyson. Only the paper mill owns more, I'll bet." My father always offered logical responses.

"I can't imagine Dad gave Gracie the land without talking it over with Mom first, so Gracie is lying through her teeth about her 'proof.' If she weren't so feeble, I might just have a go at her, woman to woman."

Dad chuckled, as he often did at Mother's silly threats. "Don't you laugh at me, Andrew!" she snapped. "I have it in me."

"I know you do, dear. I was just imagining the gossip after church if you did: 'Why, Beatrice, did you hear about Sarah knocking her own aunt off the front porch, cane and all?'" He punctuated his joke with his mock high-pitched Southern drawl.

I giggled at the vision of my mother taking someone down. The noise told them I wasn't asleep as usual on the backseat, and most of the interesting conversation drifted away. Nothing else meaningful kept me awake.

Just as we opened the front door of our home, the telephone rang, and it was Grandma. I could only hear Mother's comments like, "Of course you shouldn't, Mother...Dad never gave her that land, and you know it...There's nothing to feel guilty about. She's just a greedy woman, out to cheat her own flesh and blood...Well, I hope she drops dead!" Dad rolled his eyes at Mother's half of the conversation. Mother seemed to be on Grandma's side. I liked the sound of it.

On the occasional days when I offended my

parents, or on a day my parents fought, I would often park myself outside their thin bedroom door and eavesdrop, hoping to get a heads-up on what kind of treatment I might expect, or perhaps just to learn something of importance that I would otherwise never know. Even as an adult, before I moved into my apartment, I could hear Mother discussing her concerns with Dad. I almost think she wanted me to hear those conversations. The most disturbing tidbit of information I learned revolved around Mother's lack of respect for me and my vocation, the vocation her own father had followed.

"How could she mingle with the dregs of society? Kathleen, the cop! Can you imagine? How could she do this to herself, to us? There's a part of me that thinks I should be proud of her for doing her own thing, but the bigger part of me says it's ridiculous." Grandma had apparently never been successful at instilling in her daughter a value system based on a person's contribution to society. Mother's too often seemed based on a world where too often the clothes said more than the person underneath. I can just imagine what my uniform must have screamed.

On that last night I saw Grandma, well before I was aware of my mother's sometimes skewed value system, I decided to it would be a good night to listen in on my parents. I figured they might discuss Gracie after I had gone to bed, or at least after they believed I had. I headed down the hallway toward their room. The slant of light greeted me from beneath their door, and I knew they were still awake. Mother was discussing a side of the family history I had never heard before.

"According to Mom, before she married Dad, he and Gracie were very close. They were sure to have dinner together at least twice a week. At that time, Gracie was a secretary for a lumber company, and Dad was farming the land for the family. And even when Mom and Dad started dating, Gracie welcomed Mom. But the day Dad proposed, something clicked with Gracie, and she's been hateful ever since. Dad never knew why, and neither does Mother. Dad never forgave Gracie for distancing herself from them, and with Dad gone, things have certainly gotten worse. Maybe Gracie was just angry that Dad was moving on with his life, and she was then a lonely spinster. Now she's a lonely spinster with a bastard son. I don't know, but she can't seem to let Mom alone. And the worst part of it is, I don't know what I can do about it so far away. I'm worried to death about Mother."

"Honey, your mother is a very capable woman. I'm not the least bit worried about her. It's sad that it has to be this way, but your mom can handle it. She's survived a lot worse. Besides, if she moves near us, there really won't be much to worry about, will there? Don't be sad, darling." I couldn't hear Mother's response. And it didn't matter. My father was very good at balancing the seesaw my mother often rode. He would pull her back down to reality just at the point she seemed on the verge of floating away. Dad, with his level head and logical opinions, kept us both grounded, more or less.

As far as I knew, the only sadness that had found my grandmother was Grandpa's death. She seemed like a very jovial sort of woman, content in the home she created with her husband on the land they tended.

My parents' discussions grew more mundane, and I set out to crawl back into bed. I fell asleep easily but awoke during the night in the throes of a nightmare. I could remember no details, but I couldn't rest until I turned on my desk lamp. The white light gave me enough comfort to fall back asleep. After Grandma was killed, I was often afraid of falling asleep, that whoever had killed her would find me, that he was next door or across the street, a neighbor or a friend. I didn't want Mother to know my fears, so I would lie awake with the light on until rest found me.

Now, as I consider these conversations, it seems as though my mother may have cared for her mother, my grandmother, more than I remember. What I recall as a child was that my mother acted differently in her company—uncomfortable, out of place, or something. Maybe Mother had lost her place. Maybe she had never known it or never created it. Sometimes I feel torn between the world I'm carving out for myself and the world I think my mother tries to etch out for me. I don't know what it is that draws me deeper into a painful past that I've tried to leave buried in Alabama. Is it a search for truth and closure, or am I trying to prove myself? And if so, to whom? Myself? My mother? The ghosts of my grandparents? I have no answers.

As far as I know, Grandma didn't sell Carson Acres, although I've never heard my mother speak of it since. I write a note to myself to ask her about it. I drag out my water bottle and empty its contents into my parched mouth. I hadn't counted on leaving Grandma's house with more questions than answers, but that's what's happening. Shrouded from the sun in my hot, locked car, holding my still uneaten turkey sandwich, I sense fear I have never known, and a sadness I have chosen to forget, but I feel more alive than I have in a very long time.

## CHAPTER III

"Well, howdy, ma'am. How can I help you?" The deputy stands up awkwardly once he kicks his high-top boots off the top of the desk.

"My name is Kathleen. My grandparents, the Johnsons, lived at seventeen ninety Escambia Lane, and after they died, the house went to my mom, Sarah Johnson. Well, of course, she married. Anyway, I was just up there today and wondered if I could ask you a few questions." The adrenaline rush has carried over into my speech. I seem to be babbling.

"I'll be damned—uh, 'scuse me, ma'am. Sheriff West was talking about Sheriff Johnson just last week. Do you mind if I get him here? I'm sure he'd like to meet you."

"Sure. I'd love to talk to someone who knew my grandpa." The deputy practically jumps around his desk and grabs a handheld radio.

I have never had a problem with authority— giving it or respecting it, in law enforcement, anyway. I suppose I was destined to become a cop. Even though I was the granddaughter of a law enforcement officer, I really never knew his ways. But what must have been his unquenchable sense of curiosity—because cops by their very nature are nosy—probably tempered with a little cynicism, was part of my mother's genetic makeup, too, although she would never admit it. And what was hers became mine.

I include my mother because snooping was not

her vocation, but it certainly was and is something of an avocation. Even while reading in bed, she has her scanner tuned in, just to know what is going on around us. In public places, I grew to recognize the cues that she was eavesdropping, like her not-so-subtle "Hush, I'm listening" whispers or looks. She keeps files on people she doesn't like — notes or newspaper clippings, for what purpose I'll never know. At a pizzeria, my mother overheard what she believed to be the makings of a drug deal between an older man and a younger girl. After we paid our check, Mother rushed to an outside phone booth to contact the police. We were later told that her information led to an arrest. It was the subject of many conversations for too many months. I thought, mistakenly, that Mother's zest for intrigue, coupled with her father's work, paved the ground for me to follow. She was appalled, though, when I announced, after obtaining a college degree in journalism, that I wanted to be a street cop. "No daughter of mine will wear a gun to work. You went to school to write about the sins of others, not to catch the sinners," she spat at me. She threatened to disown me if I pursued it, but she knew I was unstoppable, and I knew she could never follow through. At least, I think she wouldn't.

"Sheriff, you aren't going to believe this, but Sheriff Johnson's granddaughter is standing right here. She's been up at the old house. Can you come in and talk to her?"

"Hell, yes!" I can hear the sheriff say. "Be there in a couple."

The deputy replaces the radio on its stand. "Excuse my manners. My name is Billy Anderson. I've been a deputy here for about three years." He bashfully sticks out his hand.

"It's nice to meet you, Billy," I respond, shaking his hearty grip. "My name is Kathleen. I'm a city cop in Jackson, Florida, myself. Been there about three years, too."

His eyes widen, as I suspected they might. "No kidding. Not very often that I meet a lady police officer." I sense a little doubt creep across his face as he sizes me up. He's about six three, 220 pounds, and I stand a full foot shorter, even in boots, and weigh more than a hundred pounds less.

"I'm tougher than I look," I say, smiling.

"I won't argue with you," he replies, finally grinning. "Probably gave them hell in the police academy, huh?"

The police academy was the highpoint of my entire academic career. I enjoyed college and journalism, but I was never drawn to it like I am to police work. I am intrigued by the laws that dictate the line between right and wrong, impressed by the defensive tactics we cops learn, and exhilarated by the weapons work at the range. On my first day at the academy, I felt amazingly comfortable in a world I had never really known. Layers of familial expectations and disappointment soon melted away, and I surprised myself and my instructors with my latent abilities and devotion to each task that came my way. One of my physical training instructors surprised me after the graduation ceremony with a rare compliment.

"I knew early on that you'd make a good cop," he said.

"Why's that, Lieutenant?" I asked, somewhat taken aback.

"That night you guys were doing PT behind the building, none of the instructors knew there were sand spurs there until some of your group started whimpering. But not you. You were even doing regular push-ups, not the ladies' version."

I knew I was going to be entering a man's world, and I wanted to make sure I was just as fit as they were. And I also knew that if my fellow students saw me work as hard as they did, I might have a chance at earning their respect. There were only three women in our group of twenty-four.

I finished the ten-month program in the top 10 percent of my class, higher than former Army Rangers and drill instructors. No one from my family came to the graduation. Grandma would have made it, though; I have no doubt about that. She would have supported me regardless of my pursuit, and she would have found this particular one honorable. It was good enough for her husband, good enough for my mother's dad. But not good enough for my own mother. However, I did find some solace in the fact that I had a job offer in Jackson, a small town adjacent to Irving. There were only seventeen officers there, and although I would start out as number eighteen, I saw that there was potential to move up the ladder, so I took the job. My aim has always been to be an investigator. Perhaps that aim is what drew me here, to Ellyson, to this mystery.

As the door swings open, the light momentarily blinds me, and when the door shuts, it is my turn to be surprised. The sheriff might be, at most, a few inches taller than I am, and I attribute that to the heels of his cowboy boots. His well-defined muscles peek out from beneath his heavily starched blue shirt.

"Sheriff Matt West. Pleased to meet you," he says, extending his hand. "So you're kinfolk of Sheriff Johnson? His granddaughter?"

"Yes, sir. I'm Kathleen Whibbs." His grip is almost too strong.

"Haven't seen any of your family in a long time, miss. I was a deputy under the sheriff who took over after your grandfather died. I met him a few times. Heard a lot of stories, like the fight he broke up between three men just by throwing dirt at them. Two of them had knives, but the sheriff had no weapon on him, so he just picked up some Alabama soil and separated them. Have I told you that one, Billy?" he asks, turning toward Billy. He shakes his head.

"Was a real good man, so I'm told." The sheriff sits down behind his worn desk and motions with a wave of his arm for me to sit down on the wooden folding chair in front of him.

"Thanks. I have a few memories of him, but I was pretty young when he died. I wish I'd had a chance to really get to know him. I miss both of my grandparents."

He cocks his head. "Really awful thing, your grandmother's murder. I still look at the case file from time to time."

The deputy pipes up, "Sheriff, she's a policewoman."

"Well, how about that! I'll be damned. Must be in the blood. What department do you work for?" He rocks back in his chair.

"The city of Jackson, sir. Three years. I'm happy to hear you still have the case file. Any chance you'd let me look at it? I was really close to my grandmother, but I was so young when she was murdered. I'd like to know more about it. My mom doesn't talk about it much."

He stands up abruptly. "Well, um, I guess there's no harm in it. If you'd like, I could make you a copy of it so you can take it with you. Not too much in it, you know." He walks with a quick gait toward a bank of filing cabinets.

"I'd be grateful, Sheriff. Is there any evidence still around?" I ask, following him. My heartbeat suddenly feels more pronounced.

"Well, yeah, funny thing about that. About two years ago, when we moved into this building from the one next door, all our stored evidence disappeared. The Johnson case and half a dozen others. They were all cold cases, but still, the evidence could have been important one day. I know there was a boot impression, tire impression, and a few other odds and ends—the quilt, maybe a rug, too. Sorry about that, Miss Kathleen."

"Oh, well," I say, "probably wouldn't have helped much after so many years." I don't let him see my disappointment.

"Billy, make a copy of this for the young lady," he says, handing him the file.

"Sure, Sheriff." Billy flips the switch on the copier over in the corner.

The sheriff returns to his desk and lights up a Marlboro red. I think he doesn't know what to say. Billy returns the original file to the sheriff and carefully staples my set together.

"I appreciate all your help, Sheriff. I just have to know all I can about it, you understand. I might come by the old house from time to time. I drive a red Mustang convertible. Can't miss me."

"You betcha. Nice to meet some young blood from an old family, Miss Kathleen. If you need anything, you let me know, you hear? Here's my card." He reaches into his front shirt pocket and draws out a creased business card. I give him mine and jot down my home number on the back.

"Thanks again, Sheriff. I really appreciate your help—and nice meeting you, Billy." He blushes, and I walk out.

I speed home, noticing neither the darkness nor the topography that so enchanted me during the drive out. I want to find some peace and quiet. There's a lot to look at—Grandma's chronicle of her life, and the investigator's chronicle of her death.

## CHAPTER IV

Surprisingly, no one is milling around the apartment complex when I drive into my parking space at home. Cops notice these things. I gather my belongings along with Grandma's, front door key ready, and head for my own threshold. I want to take a shower, wash away the past, but curiosity overwhelms me, and I sit on the floor to count the money hidden in the sackcloth. It totals $3,280. Emergency cash? I'll never really know. I shower away the cobwebs and dust and memories of my trip. With my hair wrapped in a towel, I curl up on the couch in dim light and read cover to cover Grandma's words and thoughts, all bound in her diary. Never again does she make any mention of Grandpa's death, or of any other event even remotely shrouded in mystery. My next step is to call my mother and divulge my findings. I don't know why I feel the compulsion to do that, but Grandma was her mother, and these are her things. I hesitantly pick up the phone and dial.

"Hi, Mom. How are you? I took quite a trip today." I say before she can answer. I take a deep breath, try to slow down.

"Really? Where?"

"Ellyson. I went to Grandma's house," I reply, fearful of what she might say next.

"What! Why?" Her voice rises an octave.

"Just wanted to see how things were there." I am trying, unsuccessfully, to be casual.

"You didn't get in the house, did you?" I can hear

her open the drawer that houses keys and such. She has her answer. "How was the house?" she asks in a more normal voice.

"It's been pretty much undisturbed. Of course, it's dusty and rusted and moldy. We really need to do something with it, don't you think?"

"Yes, I guess we should." Her voice falls away and is silent.

I've never been good at small talk. I even enjoy being blunt. "Did you know that Grandma hid money in her bedroom?"

Mom's response is immediate. "What! I never knew that! Where? How did you find it?"

"I found a loose floorboard next to her side of the bed. There was over thirty-two hundred dollars in a flour sack there."

"She had a savings account when she died with some money in it. I don't know; I guess she kept that for a rainy day."

Just as I thought, but that's quite a lot of rain. I am a little leery of sharing my next discovery. I have no way of knowing if she is aware of Grandma's journal. "I also found a diary—it just notes family events like births and deaths and marriages."

"I never knew she had that, either. Is there more?"

"No. That's all I found, but I did read about something in the journal I had forgotten. Grandma mentioned that Gracie offered to buy her interest in Carson Acres. I can just remember my fishing adventures with Grandpa there. What ever happened to it?"

Mother hesitates a moment. "Well, not long after Grandma died, Gracie made me an offer on the property that seemed pretty fair. We took it. I didn't see much reason to keep land in the middle of nowhere. Of course, when Gracie died, I suppose the land passed on to Cyrus, although I did hear she had been selling off her land pretty regularly to support herself." Gracie died a few years ago of cancer, so mother heard. We didn't go to that funeral.

"Oh, okay. I was just wondering."

"You don't need to concern yourself with these things, Kathleen. I let all these memories go a long time ago, and you need to, too. No good will come of this." Her discomfort is palpable over the phone line. "Leave it alone. Do you understand?"

"I know talking about Grandma's house brings you pain, and I understand why, but, Mom, I feel the need to look into her death." "Murder" is what I mean to say, but I don't want to upset her more. "To stop now would bring me pain. Doesn't it bother you, not knowing what happened or why?" I don't give her the chance to respond. "But I don't have to tell you anything I learn, unless you want me to. I really don't want to hurt you, but I have to do this. I'll bring the diary and cash to you tomorrow, and we don't have to talk about this again."

Her tone changes. She knows that when I dig my heels in, they're not coming out. "Katy, you keep the money." Just what Grandma would have said. "She would want you to have it. I just want to read the diary. Can you come over in the morning?"

"Okay. Are you sure about the money?"

"Don't mention it again, understand? I'll see you in the morning, okay?" Mom didn't ask any more about the trip, and I didn't tell about what I learned at the sheriff's office.

I hang up the phone, tentatively. I wish I hadn't told her about the diary. How will she take it, seeing a ripped-out page in the annals of Grandma's life where her birth should have been? It might hurt her, but there is nothing I can do now. And I can't understand her wanting to live out her life not knowing, assuming it's even possible to know, what happened to her mother. Maybe I would be the same way. How can I really know? Who am I to judge her?

My musings are interrupted by the sight of Grandma's money. I feel uncomfortable at having that much cash, all in twenties, in my apartment. I hide the bulk, less a few hundred I put into my wallet, in a manila envelope and place it in one of the smaller hidden compartments in the chest of drawers in my bedroom. I bought this furniture because of its secret niches. It's ironic to me that now they're hiding someone else's secret. It's a tight fit. Even out of sight, knowing it's there makes me uncomfortable.

Although I am tired, I know I will find no rest until I read the file's contents from the sheriff's office. I get out a small spiral notebook from my computer desk to take notes.

The first document is standard, similar to the one we use today: the Initial Incident Report.

The fields are complete, with her vital statistics written in legible print:

> *Full name: Emma Mae Johnson…Maiden name: Creel…Address: 1709 E. Escambia Drive, Ellyson…Telephone: 233-1886…DOB: July 31, 1916…Marital Status: Widow of Otis…Report type:* "Other" is checked off, and homicide entered onto the line. The handwriting is pretty clear, I notice. A notation on the sheet states that the investigating officer was the

Whitcomb County Sheriff, Percy Bellows. *Date: March 10, 1983...Time: 1120 hours.*

The second half of the report is an explication of the Crime Scene Report: Sheriff Bellows, lead investigator
Weather: *Clear, temp at 82*
Initial Responding Officer: *Deputy Eddy Greer, Whitcomb County Sheriff's Office*
Summons: *phone call from George Blake, delivery boy from Ida's Grocers made from the store, 155 Lee Street, Ellyson, at 1042 hours to Whitcomb Sheriff's Office.* Witness: *Body discovered by E. Greer at approximately 1052 hours.*

Victim: *Emma Mae Johnson, DOB 7/31/1916 (66 yrs.), approx. 5'5" 160 lbs, white hair, large build, found lying facedown in bed (middle bedroom). Multiple stab wounds to the back, head and neck area. Bed sheets and quilt pulled to foot of the bed. Large blood loss. Pooled blood coagulated on both sheet and floor. Arched blood splatter pattern concentrated about the headboard. No evident defensive wounds on hands, fingers or arms. Body displays extensive postmortem lividity and is cold to the touch. Appears to have been deceased for at least 12 hours. E. Greer checked for pulse and found none. Victim wearing a long, white nightgown and is barefoot. Thin gold wedding band on left ring finger. Appears victim was asleep at the time of the stabbing.*

Coroner: *William Edwards, M.D., Medical Examiners Office. Arrived on scene at approx. 1150 hours, removed victim at approx. 1400 hours to St. Christopher's Hospital morgue. Autopsy conducted. See attached report. Preliminary opinion for cause of death is multiple stab wounds to the back and neck. Time of death estimated between 2100 and 2300 hours.*

Evidence Collected: *Usable shoeprints with distinct ridges found outside mudroom door leading into dirt alleyway. Muddy shoe print inside house matches first set of prints in alleyway. Second set of shoeprints also found believed to belong to delivery boy Blake. Plaster of Paris castings of both prints made for further identification. Usable tire treads found three feet outside the back porch, then proceeding north down the alleyway. Photographs of the crime scene taken. Quilt and bed linens are taken into evidence. Blood-stained throw rug taken into evidence. Back door processed for latent prints along with door to bedroom. No additional evidence found. No additional evidence removed from house.*

Search of House: *Front door is locked. Back door is off hinges. Search of house shows no evidence or indication of robbery. Purse with wallet inside left on dining table. Wallet contains twelve dollars and 27 cents. No other room besides the second bedroom shows signs of entry. Inside bedroom, night stand objects appear undisturbed.*

Deputy Greer completed the initial incident report:

*Received call from George Blake at Ida's Grocers at approx. 1042 hours. G. Blake stated he delivered groceries to the mudroom of Emma Johnson when he noticed the door to the house off its hinges. G. Blake said he did not touch the door or enter the premises. At approx. 1059 hours, I drove down the east driveway of the Johnson residence where Mrs. Johnson's car was parked. I entered in through the back porch. The door from the mudroom leading into the house was off its hinges and propped against the frame of the door. After entering the house, I called out to Mrs. Johnson, but received no response. I checked the rooms in the front of the house and found nothing disturbed. The door to the second bedroom was shut. I knocked and called again for Mrs. Johnson, but received no response. The door was unlocked. Inside I found Mrs. Johnson facedown on her bed with what appeared to be multiple stab wounds. I found no vital signs. The rest of the room appeared undisturbed. Secured the scene and radioed for Sheriff Bellows who arrived at approx. 1115 hours.*

The follow-up interview with Blake reveals no new information. Blake willingly surrendered his boots for comparison to those at the scene. His trail matched his statement, and he was eliminated as a suspect. Interviews with neighbors offered little help. All stated that no car was reported seen or heard during that evening. According to one report, one witness stated that Gracie Jackson and Grandma were bitter enemies, but even by that time Gracie was using a walker to get around and didn't own a car. No other suspects were mentioned, and no other significant data was collected.

However, the forensic evidence did narrow the field somewhat. The boot impression clearly showed that the boot was manufactured by Chippewa, a brand widely sold throughout the state and sold out of the only store in the area that sold such items: the Ellyson Hardware Store. The ridges were not well worn, indicating the boots were not very old or not very much used. The boots were size 11 indicating that the owner was most likely between 5'10" and 6'3". The tire was a B. F. Goodrich, also widely manufactured but sold throughout the area. Markers pointed out that the treads were well worn. The murder weapon was a knife approximately five inches long. It was never recovered. The only prints recovered off the doors belonged to Grandma. No prints were found on the doorknob. Funny, I had touched at least the knob to the back of the house earlier that afternoon. The killer had to have wiped off his prints along with mine.

The autopsy was no more helpful. Given the depth of the wounds, the knife was not serrated. Could have been a hunting knife or something similar. And Grandma had apparently died quickly. End of evidence.

I see little hope of turning this information into any solution. Too little, too late. I close my notebook and decide that it, along with the case file, should be hidden away. Cops are nosy people, and because there's always a chance one could drop by, I am careful about leaving my personal information on display. Along with my important papers, my weapons, my better jewelry, and now Grandma's money, I decide to put the file and my notes in the last empty hidden compartment. As I close the drawer, I realize that the discoveries of the day have overwhelmed me, and I must seek escape, but I don't turn off the light on my nightstand tonight, and still I have a fitful night's sleep.

I wake up after eight in the morning, which is pretty late for me. I lie here, thinking about the reason why someone would want to kill Grandma. I start a pot of coffee and get the notebook out of the drawer. On the top of the first blank page, I scrawl out the word "MOTIVE." Of course, you don't have to be a cop to know that the two biggies are revenge and money. Other than Gracie, I can't imagine why anyone would ever have a reason to be angry with Grandma. As far as greed is concerned, Grandma was never wealthy, and apparently the murderer wasn't after her stash, because, according to the investigation, nothing appeared disturbed in the house except for the back door. There's always the random killing, but the killer had to work too hard, removing a door from its hinges to get in. Doesn't seem likely. Going back further, Grandpa could have put someone away who vowed revenge, but he didn't deal with too many major criminals as far as I know.

I feel the answer is somewhere in my scribblings, but I have too little information to unravel it. What I have learned reveals little about my grandmother's life and more about her death. What I saw in her was not all there was to see. She hid things, and I don't know if she hid them from herself, her husband, or someone else. The fact that she had any secrets at all is a disturbing discovery. And yet, it seems to draw me closer to her, knowing that she, too, had another side, another layer. I decide I'll have to hit the *Ellyson Gazette* and perhaps the

Whitcomb County Courthouse to do a little snooping around. I need some more background, and these landmarks seem like the best places to start.

## CHAPTER V

After scrambling eggs for breakfast, I change and head to my mother's house to drop off the diary. "I should have picked it up last night, Kathleen. I didn't get much sleep last night... You'd think Mom would have told me about the diary."

Her face suggests fear or perhaps some hurt. I doubt she'll find any consolation in the words she sees. Reading Grandma's journal last night brought me closer to her than I've been in such a long time. I felt comfort in the curve of her letters, knowing that although she was distant from me, I could still hold some part of her in my hands. I find the journal surprisingly difficult to part with. Mother takes the bound pages from me, solemnly caressing the leather cover. I know she wants to read it alone, so I quietly beg off, telling her I have errands to run. I don't tell her I'm returning to Ellyson. I guess secrets beget other secrets.

The *Gazette* is situated in the north part of town, lodged in what looks like an old brick home, isolated on a tree-lined street. Over the door is a wooden sign branded with the slogan "*Ellyson Gazette*, the News of Whitcomb County." The heavy oak door squeaks as I open it. "Hello. Lovely day, isn't it?" I remark to the middle-aged woman sitting behind the counter.

"It is indeed," she replies, looking up from her book. "What can I do for you today?" As she stands, I am struck by the pattern of her dress—very similar to one Grandma used to wear.

"I was wondering if your records go back to the 1980s, like around 1983. I had some kin who lived here, and I'm just trying to learn a little more about them. I was pretty young when they died."

"Well, sure, honey. 'Course, they're on microfilm, but I could show you how to work the machine. Any particular time in 'eighty-three, or just the whole year?" She's already busy, rifling through an old, brown filing cabinet.

"The whole year, I guess. Just curious to see what was going on around here back then." I fully anticipate her next question.

"Well, who's your kin, honey? I've been around here all my life. I might know a little myself." She looks me directly in the eye.

"Uh, the Johnsons. Lived on Escambia. I'm their granddaughter. I've come here to see about the house, so I thought I'd just learn a little more, you know…" I smile brightly and look her right back squarely in the face. "I want to find out all I can."

"Oh, well, it is important to know where you came from. I can tell you come from good stock, though. Shame what happened to them." Her face has lost its humor. She pulls out a reel with "1983" typed on a label across its center. "Come over here, honey, and I'll get you started. By the way, my name's Beatrice, but people around here call me Bea."

"Thanks for your help, Bea. My name's Kathleen." She sets the reel in the antiquated steel viewer and pulls over a heavy, well-worn oak chair on casters and makes me sit down.

"You just use this little knob here to advance the film. Nothin' to it." I give it a practice turn, and she pats me on the shoulder and bounds off to another room. "I'm getting some coffee, fresh-made. Can I get you a cup?"

"Thanks, Bea." After bringing me the too-sweet coffee in the Styrofoam cup, she politely returns to reading her book. We sit in silence except for the squeaky noise of the reel that tells Bea I'm still looking.

I scan mostly headlines, nothing too earth-shattering: MCABEE'S FARM HAS RECORD YEAR,...EVERMAN SON KILLED ON VACATION,...TRAIN DERAILMENT DESTROYS DEPOT PLATFORM. I read, word for word, every article written about Grandma's murder, but nothing important appears that I haven't already read in the police reports. After March, nothing I see catches my eye until I almost skip over a story, WHITCOMB COUNTY THOUGHT TO BE OIL RICH." The article, dated April 23, 1983, stops my hand from moving forward.

> *American Petroleum & Refining Company has leased in excess of 10,000 acres in Whitcomb County following their oil discovery near Turkey Creek. It is rumored that the well is capable of producing in excess of 800 barrels of oil daily. Scores of oil men, both from major companies and independent wildcatters, have filled all the nearby motels. They are competing with American in leasing and have caused lease prices to exceed $500 per acre...*

The article goes on to interview landowners, some of whom hope to "strike it rich" or "never have to punch a card again." One American representative is quoted as saying the area could be worth several million to the royalty owners alone. The details on the location of the leases are sketchy, but nevertheless I make notes to check this information at the courthouse. *Could Carson Acres play a part in this?* My foray through the microfilm continues without significant discovery. I thank Bea for her guidance, pack it in, and head for the heart of the county seat.

The third largest building on the square, overshadowed only by the churches, was built with an optimism that never came to fruition. Too grand, really, adjacent to run-down businesses and vacant storefronts, the courthouse is fronted with a well-manicured lawn and blooming azaleas. The edifice is carpeted with marble stairs and hallways that lead to quiet rooms. I pass through the metal detector without notice, having left my weapon and badge under the front seat of my car. I ask the security guard wearing a stained uniform shirt the directions to the probate office. He points toward the next hallway. "Take a left there. First door on the right," he tells me, and I sense his stare as I walk away.

The "Take a Number" sign seems out of place in this office where I'm the only visitor. Both ladies behind the half windows look up as I enter, and one smiles. "How can I help you?" she inquires, happy with the intrusion.

"I hope you can. I'm a courthouse novice. I'm looking for some old records, leases I suppose, that were filed in middle to late 'eighty-three. I don't know where to start." Calling myself a novice isn't quite fair. My father's job while I was a teenager often involved courthouse work in Florida. I would often accompany him.

"That's why we're here, hon." Everyone says "hon" here. She opens the door next to her and draws me into the back. "If you know the name of the grantor or grantee, you can use the index books to run it down. Do you know what month in 1983 you need?" She walks toward a row of yellow metal bookshelves that house thickly bound books, capped by a sign that reads, "Land Records Room."

"No, I really don't. I suppose I'll just have to thumb through the grantor index."

She directs me to the applicable books, and I take down the volume that includes the alphabetical listing of grantors, A to K. I quickly flip to the J's and then to Johnson. I find that Gracie had granted two oil, gas, and mineral leases to American Petroleum, recorded in book 227, on pages 191–95. These transactions were recorded on June 17, 1983, just over three months after Grandma was killed. By the legal description I don't recognize either of these properties as Carson Acres, so I reverse my work. Grandma was killed in March 1983, and Mother sold her interest in the land shortly thereafter, so I begin looking in May of that year in the other volume, L–Z, looking for Whibbs. Cross-referencing the legal descriptions, I learn that, indeed, what was Grandma's interest in Carson Acres was leased to American soon after her death.

My head begins to reel. Could Gracie have known about American before the April newspaper article? Makes sense. Gracie was a pretty big landowner, so she probably was contacted early on. She wasn't content with her half interest in that property for some reason, but Grandma didn't want to sell. Gracie wanted it all. Grandma is murdered, and Gracie buys the property from the unsuspecting heirs. Gracie was greedy, greedy enough to kill her family. Can't be. No, no, I'm jumping to conclusions. Certainly, it could be possible, but no, it really can't. I suddenly feel sick. Anyway, Gracie was incapable of murdering Grandma. She was much too feeble. She would have needed help.

As I walk out of the probate office, my body is numb. This can't be right. It can't be family. But it makes sense, a very sick sort of sense. I hear the clack, clack of my sandals on the hard floor as I make my way to the exit. The same security guard stands by the door, and his eyes never leave me. *In your dreams,* I think to myself.

Dreams—I was certainly good at dashing Mother's. During my childhood and youth, she and I often didn't speak, once for nearly a week. I think she was always surprised to find me to be as stubborn as she. Her anger almost always stemmed from disapproval, not that I was doing anything so bad, but I wasn't doing the prissy stuff she hoped I would. She thought I would make a great cheerleader; I thought I made a better hurdler. I even made it to the track regionals, but neither of my parents had the time to come to the meet. That's one of the times I didn't speak to her. Somehow I always forgave my father more easily. I often felt as though he followed Mother's lead just to keep the peace. Or maybe not. But my mother has always been more vocal in pointing out what she perceived to be my mistakes. I was supposed to be a junior miss like she was, but I preferred taking flying lessons with my dad, a private pilot. I wasn't the kind of daughter she wanted, and moreover, I wasn't going to do anything about it. She had difficulty accepting that, and I suppose she still does. But I try not to worry about the things I can't control. It dawns on me that ironically, playing "Miss Kathleen" today, I am probably as close to my mother's ideal version of me as I ever have been. I realize that I have not found the pretense completely empty of pleasure, and the realization brings me some shame.

I pull myself back into the realm of things I can

control, to the person I really am, and decide that I need to document all that I learn. I am not comfortable sharing my hypothesis with anyone until I find the proof that I believe will lead me to Gracie. Once home, I pull out the notebook again and write these words: my memories, my guesses, my log of evidence that will, I hope, take me somewhere I can learn the truth.

## CHAPTER VI

My weekend, well, what I call two days off in a row, has been so mentally taxing that it is difficult for me to return to work. I report in on time and find some comfort in seeing Joe's smiling face and Atlas's wagging tail. "Hey, bud. How was your weekend?" I call to him from across the dispatch office.

"Busy. I worked on my house all weekend — laid tile in the guest bathroom. What about you?" he asks as he glances over the last two days of call logs.

"Oh, just spent most of my time with family, you know." I don't know why I'm hesitant to tell him I mean my deceased family, my family skeletons. I am surprised at my discretion. Joe's opinion means a lot to me. I have never told him about this past of mine, and for some reason, I'm afraid he'd look at me differently, more as the victim's family than as the problem solver I'm supposed to be on these streets. Foolish, I know. Atlas lumbers over to me, and I scratch the nape of his neck, his favorite spot for affection.

"Damn, we missed an armed robbery last night down at B & B Furniture. Says the suspects were carrying automatics. You better read the BOLO before we head out tonight. Be on the lookout for a brown four-door sedan. What else is new?" Joe walks into the patrol room to get his 800 radio, a scrambled-frequency transmitter that can't be picked up on scanners.

He made the comment about the four-door sedan because if a witness isn't sure of the make and model, the description always seems to default to a brown sedan. Joe returns with a radio for me. "I've got eight," he tells me, so that I can radio him if the need arises. "Chief says we need to work Belvedere a while today."

"Got it. Meet you on there in twenty?" I ask, not shielding my disappointment but knowing we both need time to fill up our patrol cars.

"Sounds like a plan, man." He ambles out with Atlas bouncing at his heels. Atlas loves to work. I glance at the current BOLOs and jot down a few notes of makes and models and descriptions of perps.

"If you need anything, Wendy, let me know." Wendy is our favorite dispatcher. She goes beyond the job and digs a little deeper than the others we have. She's conscientious about keeping up with ten-four safety checks when we're out on calls, too. It's nice to know someone's looking out for us.

"You guys have fun. Well, not too much, you know. I like it kinda quiet," she says with a wink.

My field training officer, or FTO, Joe Carpenter, never was comfortable with keeping things quiet. He's still that way today. Joe was a bastard to me at first, but he has my respect because of his command of the law and his sixth sense that leads to many arrests. He is also the K-9 officer of his German shepherd, Atlas. Joe taught me early on that there's a great distance between understanding the law and being able to make crucial decisions about what's happening in a matter of a seconds or, when we're lucky, minutes. The former is education, the latter interpretation. I stumbled a lot in the beginning, and Joe was quick to point out my errors, but he made me a better officer. "What kind of officer safety was that, Kathleen? You've got to stay back of the driver's window unless you want to get blown away!" I felt like such an idiot so many times. "You're too slow on the radio, Kathleen. Spit it out and get off."

The first time I positively impressed him — although he didn't admit it until a couple of years later — occurred about three weeks into my training. We were riding around the high school about 9:00 p.m. when he spotted a suspect trespassing on the otherwise empty property. We drove toward him, and as we neared, he took off on foot. Without thinking or asking, I opened the passenger door and sprang out after him. He ran up and down the covered sidewalk maze outside the locked buildings as I tried to give out my location from my shoulder mike during the pursuit. Finally we emerged from the web of concrete into an open space — the parking lot on the other side of the building. Joe was standing there, leaning against his patrol car, waiting for him, all smug and relaxed. The trespasser came to a full stop, Joe grabbed one of his arms, and I grabbed the other, and that was that. After Joe led me through the paperwork, and we returned to patrol, he admonished me. "You showed good initiative, Kathleen, but you're supposed to be observing me, not doing your own thing. Something could have gone wrong. You got lucky." I thought I detected a smile under the harsh words. I couldn't share with him the sense of euphoria I felt at chasing the runner down and helping to catch a lawbreaker, albeit a minor one. It was my first pursuit, and I knew I had made the right decision to be a cop.

Joe's attitude toward me seemed to ease up after that night, and I completed my training without any major errors or damage – property or personal. I have suffered two minor injuries, however, one of which occurred while working with a different training officer during the day shift. Walter and I drove down a known drug-dealing street. He noticed a guy walking toward an apartment and recognized him.

"That's Jack Sebastian. He's got an active warrant. Let's get him." One thing about Walter: he knew everyone on the street—all the ones in trouble, anyway. Once Jack noticed us, I could see his body tense up. We cut off his access to the apartment door.

"Hey, man, what's the problem? I'm just going home."

"I know, Jack. Just want to make sure everything's okay. Haven't seen you around lately," Walter said as we closed in on him. Jack looked at Walter and then at me, and sensing the danger of dealing with us, he took off. I tried to get in front of him, but he pushed me to the ground with such force that he knocked the wind out of me. I got up as quickly as I could and ran after Walter, who was running after Jack. Jack eventually gave up the race—fatigued, I guess—and Walter and I proceeded with the arrest and added a few other charges, like battery on a law enforcement officer.

"Kathleen, you're never going to stop a train from moving by getting in front of it. You're going to have to outsmart them sometimes—trip them up, come at them from the side." Walter looked at me with a faint air of disgust. I was disappointed with myself, but I learned another lesson. Joe teased me when he heard about it.

"You're not as strong as you think you are. How are you going to stop a car? Stand in front of it? Use that brain, lady!" Knowing that Joe's opinion of me had dropped a notch or two did little for my ego, but he eventually forgave me.

My other injury caused me even more embarrassment. Working on a bike patrol had always sounded appealing to me, and although we have a small department, our chief is interested in taking advantage of all the tools of the police trade. He sent me and another officer to bike patrol school at a neighboring department. The classroom instructions and patrol techniques proceeded uneventfully until we had to ride trails in a forest. Not wanting to be outdone by the men in the class, I raced ahead toward the front of the group, but I lost control of my bike and plunged headfirst into a tree. I was briefly knocked out, so they told me, but the real injury was from a small piece of broken branch deeply imbedded in my leg. I pulled it out without thinking and was surprised at how little it bled.

All the guys tried to play hero and offered to pick me up and carry me out to a clearing. But as they held me over the uneven terrain, I was more worried about being dropped than using my damaged leg, so I had them put me down. Worse yet, someone radioed over the airwaves "officer down," which drew out all kinds of emergency vehicles and the chief of the police department. He insisted that I go the emergency room, which I did, but they did little more than clean the wound. I thought my fellow officers would give me a hard time about it, but — to my face anyway — they only expressed concern.

"Good thing you weren't alone, Kathleen," Joe said the next day.

"Ha, wish I'd been alone," I responded. I didn't like the others seeing me in need.

When I was finally assigned my own patrol car, Joe came up to me and said, "When you started here, I thought I was going to have to fail you out of the program. But you really surprised me, Kathleen. You might make a damn good cop if you work at it — at least half as good as I am," he said, laughing. I had been accepted.

Behind the wheel of my own patrol car, I soon learned how I liked to spend my shift. With such a small department, on most days there are only two officers on duty at any one time. I requested and got the evening shift, the one where I could frequently work with Joe. I don't especially enjoy working as a traffic cop, writing speeding and parking tickets, but I do love to patrol the drug areas and snoop around looking out for the more serious crimes and criminals, the deals and dealers. Joe prefers that kind of work, too, so we often work together to check out the heavy drug areas and the cars that visit them. Joe is two years older than I am, and I think of him as my older brother. He's tall and physically fit, has dark brown hair and eyes—boyish, certainly attractive, but I don't really see him in that way. He has a girlfriend, but I know that if I need him, he'll be there for me. During many of his nights working, Joe is accompanied by a reserve officer, Pat, a good ol' boy who grew up in Jackson and knows many of the local characters.

The beauty of the evening shift is that you have it all. The first part of my work day begins during regular civilian working hours. We patrol businesses, run a little radar, answer the occasional call. But at night, the whole dynamic changes. People start to drink or use drugs and lose control of themselves or their vehicles; angry spouses meet up at home after work; kids are out of school. The blinds drop down, and my lights blink on. I'm pretty sure my world is not my grandfather's. I doubt that he saw the things I see, like the man who decided to kill himself with a shot to the temple carved out with his newly bought .45. I doubt Grandpa even saw an illegal drug or a badly beaten spouse. I don't know what draws me to this work, but I like it when my world shifts.

Maybe I was sheltered too long, growing up in a cocoon of sorts, free from the tarnish of this sometimes darker world. As I mull over these why-am-I-here possibilities, I realize that Joe is probably waiting for me to fill up my car and meet him.

Belvedere is a street in a residential neighborhood where speeding is often a problem and a concern to the parents whose children have to cross the street to get to the public park. Apparently our chief received a number of complaints recently because he left Joe a note to run a little radar there to slow things down. Joe likes to clock the speeds, and I do the ticket writing. He's senior to me, so I have to live with it.

"About time. First day back at work and already you're slacking," he admonishes as I drive up to his window.

"I am not. I was taking notes on the BOLOs, mister. You're the one who's slacking." He laughs at my accusation. We're always razzing each other.

"Jennifer wants to meet us for dinner at Lou's. I'll have to call her with a time." Jennifer is Joe's girlfriend. She's both attractive and a lot of fun to be around. I am currently without a love life, not that this is so unusual, and Joe's always pointing out men for me to pursue. It appears that he doesn't have very good taste—in men, anyway, or at least the kind that would interest me. Besides, most of the ones we meet aren't exactly the kind I could take home to meet my mom. Certainly not the ones in handcuffs.

"Sounds good. But you know, now that you have plans, we'll damn sure get a call."

"I know, but you gotta try, right?" He smiles, not at his feeble joke but at the car whizzing up the hill. "Fifty-five in a thirty-five. Go get 'em, girl."

Traffic enforcement bores me, and Joe knows it. We cite five more vehicles over the next hour and a half and decide that we've had enough. We've had no calls during that period, which isn't so unusual. I patrol the closing businesses and head back to the station. Joe is there, waiting for a call from Jennifer about a time to meet for dinner.

While we're chatting with the dispatcher, a 911 call comes in. Wendy takes notes and hangs up the phone. "We've got another fight at the Veazy residence. Ricky's been drinking and is apparently throwing dishes or glasses around the house. Neighbor says they're making quite a racket."

Joe and I are very familiar with this house. Ricky is Ann's son, and he frequently loses control, usually after a six-pack of generic beer. Joe and I quickly get out to our police cars and head over.

The front door of the small red-brick house hangs wide open, and getting out of my vehicle, I can hear screams echoing out the breach: "Damn it, Mama. What the hell you doing making pies for people and not bothering to make me, the man who brings money home, something for dinner! Every day it's the same damn thing, Mama." I hear another piece of glass shatter inside.

"Hey, Ricky, it's Officer Whibbs. Come out here for a minute." Joe is creeping toward the back of the house.

"What the hell! Did one of them damn nosy neighbors call you? Which one was it?" I still can't see him, and I'm careful to avoid the doorway and any possible projectiles that might fly out.

"Come out, Ricky. We gotta talk. No sense in wasting any more of my time."

"See what you do to me, Mama? *Damn* you!"

Ricky stumbles outside as I wait for him just to the left side of the front door, just out of his view. I snatch him quickly and pat him down for weapons as he braces himself against the house. Contrary to his norm, he doesn't resist or even fight me.

I radio to Joe, "Got him up front." Joe comes back around the house and proceeds to talk to him as I check on his mom. "You okay Mrs. Veazy?" There is broken glass and dinnerware all over the kitchen and dining room. She is crying softly.

"I don't know how I raised such a creature. I bake an apple pie for Mr. Potts—he has cancer, you know—and that makes me bad. I just don't understand him. It's that damn liquor, I guess. It ruined his father, too." She seems so pitiful, seated on a split red-covered vinyl barstool. I notice a couple of small trickles of blood on one of her arms.

"You're bleeding a little bit, Mrs. Veazy. Are you hurt anywhere else?" I ask as I approach her.

"No, just in my heart. He didn't hit me. These little nicks ain't anything. Nothing he does to the outside of me is like the pain I feel on the inside." She buries her face in her arthritic hands.

"What do you want us to do with him, Mrs. Veazy? Should he go to Steve's?" Steve is Ricky's only friend, as far as I know.

"Yes, I think that would be a good idea. I've got a lot of cleaning to do." She looks up to assess the damage.

"You know what, Mrs. Veazy? I think he should have to clean it up himself. I'm going to stand here while he does it, too. Is that all right with you?" I see a subtle smile creep up on her face.

"I reckon. How you gonna get him to do that?"

"Leave it to me," I tell her.

Convincing Ricky poses a greater challenge. "Hell, no, I won't! She *made* me do it, I tell you!"

"Let me put it to you this way, Ricky," I say in a softly menacing tone, "If you don't, I will just arrest you for criminal mischief. You could have really hurt your mother throwing glass all around her. As it is now, she's bleeding." He glances up at me; I stare back.

"Damn it," he mumbles, and I follow him into the house.

At about this time, dispatch calls about an audible alarm at Quincy Automotive—a frequent occurrence anytime we have more than a gentle breeze. Joe responds, and I am left to supervise Ricky's cleanup work.

By the time I leave the Veazy house, I figure it's too late to expect to eat with Joe and Jennifer, so I run through a fast food drive-through, and choke down yet another cheeseburger supper while I'm parked in a nearby bank parking lot. Listening to nothing more than the stream of Diet Coke move up my straw as I absently replay Ricky and his mama's conversations in my head, something occurs to me: Gracie's son, Cyrus.

I know little about him except his name. I remembering seeing him in a picture, but I couldn't describe a thing about him. I don't know what he does for a living or what became of him, but something tells me I must try to find out. Unlike Ricky, some sons would do anything for their mothers. I could use the resources available to me at the PD to search for him, but I try very hard not to step over the line between what's okay and what's not—and unauthorized access is most definitely not, so I decide to try my luck over the Internet at home. I quickly finish my drink and head to my apartment to use the computer.

I try a variety of search engines but don't get any hits on a Cyrus Johnson in Alabama. I try Mississippi, too, but am unsuccessful there. When I enter "C. Johnson" in Alabama, however, I get several hits, one of whom lives in Ellyson. *Likely,* I think to myself. I jot down the listed telephone number and address and stick the note in my shirt pocket. Now that I have this information, I'm not sure what to do with it.

The rest of our shift proceeds uneventfully, and I am quick to go off duty. Once home again, I pull out my notebook and jot down my notes to bring everything up to date. The next page I title "SUSPECT." Because I don't remember (assuming I ever knew) where Gracie lived, I have no way of knowing if C. Johnson's address is the same. I rifle through the paperwork I've collected thus far for the pages containing the interview with someone who mentions Gracie. Unfortunately, it doesn't give her street address. Tomorrow I will return to Ellyson before my shift and do a little more snooping in the courthouse. I know my mother would disapprove. Not only am I digging in a covered family grave, but I'm also exposing our family's private affairs while playing a role my mother hates: cop. But something tells me that she wants to know what happened as much as I do, that when we share the truth, she may see that I have disappointed her far less than she feared.

## CHAPTER VII

Although my shift doesn't begin until 2:00 p.m., my alarm is set for 6:30—yet I am up well before that remembering a kind of nightmare, a distortion of an arrest I helped make a few months ago after a felon fled from a clapboard house and disappeared into a nearby swamp.

What I can't seem to forget was how hard it was to be quiet when I needed to. I tried to stand noiselessly, but it only made my heart beat louder, my breathing more labored. I could feel the sweat rolling down my cheek onto my shirt in this expanse of humidity in the swamp, but I couldn't wipe it away. This steaming summer evening, as deputies tried to serve a warrant for aggravated battery, the felon fled out the back door of the house where he was staying. He ran out shoeless and shirtless into the swampland that began just yards outside the back door. Joe and Atlas were called on the radio to assist in the chase; I followed as backup. During our heated drive to the location, I noticed how quickly the landscape shifted from businesses and homes to nothingness. The only lights on either side of the two-lane road were those that illuminated our drive.

A rustic home, the scene of the escape, stood among tall pines, isolated from the street by a long dirt driveway. As we drove up, I noticed a woman with a small mixed-breed dog by her side, both of whom appeared focused on the swampland. The mutt yapped at us as we got out of our patrol cars.

"You need to put that dog up. I'll be letting my K-9 out," Joe warned her.

"He can stand his own," she replied with a sneer. She was a heavy woman in a pink housedress, standing barefoot on the grassless ground.

Joe retrieved Atlas's lead from the trunk of his patrol car and stepped to the backseat. Atlas was in constant bark mode, either in anticipation of a search or from the residual excitement of their drive. Whatever the cause, Atlas was persistent. When he jumped out of the car, the woman immediately scooped up her dog and took it inside the house. Once out of the car, Atlas stopped barking. Everything, including the keyed-up shepherd, grew still.

The darkness here was different, different from my bedroom at home with all the lights turned off. Here the night was murky, torpid, as if weighed down by the heavy, sweaty vegetation. Too quiet. I heard neither crickets nor birds. Too dark, with no moon and a cloud cover partially blotting the stars.

Flashlights at the ready, we were set to embark on our search for the fugitive. The deputy identified the felon's point of entry into the swamp, where he most likely stepped, an imperative starting point for a K-9 scent track. Before we started out, however, Joe called out, "Police! Come out, or I will release my dog!" He repeated the warning, but only silence responded. Atlas was pulling so hard on the lead, he nearly choked himself.

The demarcation between yard and swamp was definitive. Around the house, even around the driveway, the land had been cleared. But for a few widely spaced trees, the settled part was blank space; on the other side, however, there loomed a curtain of tangled shadows.

We penetrated this drape. At first Joe kept Atlas on lead, but because the underbrush stood so thick, the tether posed a menace to both dog and handler. Once off lead, Atlas made better progress in this uninhabitable space. Joe ran close behind him, and I brought up the rear.

Because it was so dark, and because Atlas stayed several strides ahead of us, I couldn't always keep him in view. I could see Joe, though, and although I tried to duplicate his movements, threading through the labyrinth of foliage, stepping in his steps, ducking where he ducked, I seemed to find new obstacles to wade through that he never seemed to notice.

When I could see Atlas, his nose was low, sniffing the ground off our left flank and then to our right. Later Joe explained that Atlas had lost the track and was trying to pick the scent back up. Our serpentine-like search continued for at least an hour, our paths over broken limbs and thick vines. Other times, just to make room to walk, we carved out space with our flashlights, our blunt machetes, banging our way through the briars.

We rarely used our flashlights for their designated purpose, trying not to give the felon a spotlighted target in case he was armed. During one of the few times Joe scanned around us with his Maglite, a dense canopy of branches stretched overhead. I wondered if this invisible man was there, lurking among the limbs, laughing to himself about how clumsily we hunted below.

Joe gave intermittent commands to both Atlas and me for "quiet." Under the dense trees and mired in the thick undergrowth of this swampy, unpopulated, uncivilized area, the briars and creepers seemed to entangle each step we took, so trying to move in unison was futile. Sometimes we would hear a distinctive noise—a snap of a limb, a rustle of a tree—and hurry off in that direction, but the sound led us nowhere; Atlas could pick up no track. At each of Joe's commands for quiet, I froze, trying to be noiseless on command and hearing little more than Atlas's panting and my own heartbeat. When we stood rigid, I hoped to hear some telling sound, and stifled, my senses sought for any stimulation. The fireflies were the only stars that night. The mysterious way they suddenly appeared and then blinked out just at the moment I focused my eye on them gave the night even greater intrigue. Not that I could consider them a source of light, but when my eyes searched for anything in the blackness that enveloped us, I couldn't help but be drawn to them.

Time stretched on as we trekked in the darkness of the swamp. Although at times I had difficulty keeping Joe or Atlas in view, the sounds of their movement were easy to track: off to the right walking, straight ahead running, stopping, turning, resting, listening.

After more than an hour of false starts and stops, Joe called the search off, and we turned to retrace our steps to the beginning of the maze. But during all the running and turning and backtracking, we had lost all sense of direction. No light nor sound nor landmark was visible; no familiar noise beckoned us back. No trails were evident. Every pine and cypress looked like every other. Each broken limb looked like the last. The terrain showed no foot prints, absorbing every track in the muck. "Unit nine to Hatton. Tap your horn. We're having trouble finding our way out." The honk sounded so far away.

As we made our way back through the dense net of vegetation, neither of us talked, silenced by fatigue and discouragement. Walking back, I began to strip off all the intensity that had maintained me during the search — anxiety, expectation, heightened senses — and I loosened my concentration. I then began to realize how dry my mouth was, how much my neck ached, how soaked with sweat I was. I numbly followed Joe, who seemed to be numbly following Atlas in the direction of the house. I don't remember seeing anything but Joe's silhouette and the beams of our flashlights as we made our way back.

When we finally emerged from the tangle of dampness, Atlas began darting left and right, searching for a track. At first I thought he was backtracking toward the house, picking up nothing more than the beginning route of the felon's run. But the direction he took was not the one we had followed.

Suddenly, before Joe and I could catch up to him, I heard Atlas growl softly. All that energy that I had abandoned in the swamp came back in one charging moment. We ran toward the growl and found a man laying facedown behind some bushes near the house. He was tall and thin, wearing only a pair of faded blue jeans, conspicuously hiked up at the point where Atlas was tugging on them.

"Get your hands behind your back!" Joe yelled at him.

"Get your dog off me, and I will!" he barked back.

"Dog doesn't come off until your hands are behind your back," Joe explained.

He complied, slowly sliding his hands down from around his head. Joe called Atlas off, and I cuffed the suspect while Joe showered Atlas with accolades. "Good boy," he kept saying, "good boy." By his own admission, the man had run into the swamp but had looped around and backtracked behind us and waited by the house, hoping we would give up and go home. We had — almost. But Atlas never did.

After the felon was secured in the backseat of the deputy's car, Joe looked Atlas over for injuries. Except for general fatigue and mud up to his haunches, he was in good condition. Considering how dehydrated I was, I knew Atlas had to be suffering. Sensing that, too, Joe immediately got out the half-full water bowl from the car, which the dog greedily lapped up. Both Joe and I had minor scrapes along our arms and faces that we had never felt or noticed till now. A tell-tale sprig of mallow was wedged tightly into my gun belt. Our boots were filthy.

Standing next to my patrol car in that desolate expanse in these visions of dream-like truth, I am suddenly struck with a fleeting vision of my grandmother, asleep in her bed the night she was killed. Perhaps the similarity in the two houses had awakened my buried memories of that horrid night so many years ago. I shook off the chill of the hunt, the sweat of the find.

But the heat of that night has followed me home, to my grandmother's home. I have tried to keep the nightmare of that day submerged, and now I am suddenly overwhelmed with the horror of it. I have not allowed myself to wallow in how much I missed Grandma: her kindness, her unconditional love. As I lean against my pillow, I am struck by the connection of these two houses: one a vision in my nightmare, one a vision in my dreams; one whose flecked paint housed a criminal and one whose flecked paint housed a crime. I know in my bones that the memories of that dreadful night can never be reburied. I know that I have to do something…I have to do something. Now. I fix a quick piece of toast and head to the shower while my coffee brews.

Armed with a spill-proof coffee mug, I'm off by eight and make it to the Whitcomb County Courthouse stairs shortly after ten. I walk right past the probate office and head to the tax assessor's office to find out Gracie's address back in the eighties. I learn that, unlike the land records, homestead records are more readily accessible. With a quick thank-you, I pass on an offer of help from one of the women and head to the shelf containing the year and alphabetical listing of the early 1980s. Within a few minutes, I confirm that Gracie, back then, and C. Johnson, now, share the same address. Still, I reason, this doesn't necessarily mean anything. I'm operating on a hunch, and a hunch is a good place to start, but never a place to end. The physical evidence is paltry, but it's something at least. I already know from the police report that the shoe print comes from a Chippewa, a brand of boot that was once sold in town. That same hardware store is still open. I have about two more hours to do some checking, and although I doubt that I could be so lucky, I decide to take the chance.

Ellyson Hardware is only commercial building on the center square that looks as though it's been somewhat maintained. The hardware store's ruddy red paint stands in stark contrast to the dull grays and tans of other buildings on the street. It would be unreasonable, I surmise as I open the front door, to think that they would for any reason maintain records of who bought what way back when. Even if there were such a record, on its own, it would confirm nothing, at least as far as the prosecutor's office might be concerned. But for me it's a different story—I could learn a lot.

"Howdy, ma'am. What can I do for you today?" The salesclerk, in his late teens, is dwarfed by the floor-to-ceiling homemade wooden shelves that house a variety of boots. I doubt that he will have the information I need, so I ask for the owner.

"Well, I need some information about this store from many years ago. I don't suppose the owner's around today?" I smile brightly at him.

"Nah, he don't come down here much. He's my pop. Had a heart attack a while back, and Ma and I take care of the store for him." I recognize more maturity in his nature than I had expected. Age can often be deceptive.

"Sorry to hear that. You might be able to help me, then. I know this is a crazy question, but did you keep any records of who bought what, say, about seventeen years ago? And if you did, do you still have those records?" The more I speak, the more foolish I feel.

"I know we have a lot of old records from charge accounts we billed monthly. I don't know how far they go back, but they're in the attic. We probably should throw them out—a fire hazard and all—but my pop says you never know when you might need something. Mind me asking what you're looking for?" He doesn't appear suspicious, merely curious.

"Well, I'm a police officer, and I'm working on an old crime. I've traced some evidence back to this town and maybe even this store. I need to find out who may have bought some Chippewa boots. I'd be very grateful if you could share those records with me." I think that in telling him part of what I want, I might gain an eager research associate.

"No way!" His eyes open wide. "Sure, I'll give you what we got. I've got a little free time, too, if you'd like some help." He is already heading toward the back of the building.

"That would be wonderful. I can use all the help I can find. What's your name, by the way?" I step quickly to keep up with him.

"It's David, David Early. Pleased to meet you."

"I'm Officer Whibbs, but you can call me Kathleen."

"I like 'Officer' better," he says with a smile as he looks back at me over his shoulder.

David feels above the door frame, and his hand emerges with a key which he uses to unlock the door. We walk up the stairs to a partially finished attic laden with boxes. I am relieved to see they have been labeled by year, but I am fearful that 1983 has long ago been tossed.

"Do you know what year you need?" he asks, blowing the dust from a box top.

"I think 1983 would be a good place to start." I am more hopeful now as I make out "1981" scrawled in pencil on the cardboard box in his hands.

"'Eighty-three? I was still in diapers."

"Gee, thanks for the reminder," I chuckle in response.

"Here's 1982, and '83's right beside it. This must be your lucky day."

"You're not kidding. I didn't really expect to find it here. You can't imagine what a help you are!" Even in the fluorescent light I can see him blush.

"The box is pretty light," he says as he picks up the records. "I'll just carry it downstairs, and we can go through it down there, if you like, that is."

"Sounds like a great idea. I sure appreciate your help."

David travels down the stairs as quickly as he went up, and, within a minute, he places the box on an oversized table fashioned from part of a barn door. "You said Chippewa, right? You know the style or size?" He removes the lid, and I am thrilled to see the box only half full.

"I don't know the style, but it was a size eleven. Hope that narrows it down a little."

"We sell quite a few elevens, and if the perp was a cash customer, we'll never find him."

I see David has been watching a little reality TV. I sense that he is a potential ally and junior investigator, so I encourage his interest. "If his record's in there, I'll bet you'll be the one to find it, David." His grin is infectious.

Each postcard-sized paper has yellowed with age, and many of the records have been sprinkled and stained with the hardened waste of some animal, probably cockroaches. David doesn't seem to notice and picks up each record carefully, inspects the somewhat-legible handwriting and promptly replaces the rejects. I begin working from the opposite end, which, I quickly see, begins with December — well after the murder.

"Hey, David, do you mind if we switch sides, and you can work backwards from the end of the year?"

"Sure, no problem." He points out where he has left off.

David is still in the month of January. The invoices are detailed enough, most giving brand name, style and size, date of charge, and the person responsible, as well as the price. I thumb through them quickly, and not until the end of January do I find something interesting: Chippewa, size 11, sold January 30 to Gracie Johnson. I am stunned — so stunned that I don't even notice David calling out to me. Finally I remember his presence when he touches my hand as I hold the invoice above the box.

"Officer Whibbs, Officer Whibbs! Are you okay?

Did you find it? Did you find something?" He is leaning across the table, trying to look at the card.

"I might have, David." I try to contain myself. "But to be a good investigator, you have to go beyond the obvious. We've got to search the whole year to see if any others were sold. It's our duty." I am sure that I am pale.

"Oh, right. Of course. I'll keep looking." I can see the excitement building in his face. Within five minutes he screams out, "I got one! I got one! Size eleven Chippewa, sold to the McMann family."

"What's the date, David?"

"August fifteenth." He hands me the card.

I don't have the heart to tell him it's too late, so I take it from him and carefully read it over. "Great work, partner. You're doing a super job here. I may have to deputize you." He blushes again. "Let's keep looking, though, okay?" I put the card over the one I already pulled.

He resumes his efforts without a word. I continue riffling through the cards, still overwhelmed with my discovery. I peel back each one, no longer expecting more than I already have. David and I nearly meet in May when I notice another charge to the Johnson household. It's another size 11 shoe, but a different brand altogether. I promptly pull it out and add it to my pile. David just looks at me. I don't say a word. If Cyrus had heard that the police recovered a boot print, he may have been worried and ditched his Chippewas just to be safe. He would have to replace them. Why else would he buy two pairs of boots within four months? I decide that I need to look over the whole year again to see what had been charged to the Johnson family and when, and not only for that year, but for the years before and after 1983.

"David, you've been a great help. I think I've

found what I came looking for, but I need to do a little more research. Would you mind bringing the years 1982 and 1984 down for me, so I can finish up my work?"

"Well, sure. I'll get them for you." He looks downcast.

While he's gone, I call work on my cell phone. "Hey, girl. It's me. I'm out of town, and I won't make it back before my shift starts. Can you call the lieutenant and let him know? Hate to do this on such short notice, but I just can't get back in time." I do feel the weight of guilt. I've never missed work except for illness.

Once my newfound ally returns with the boxes, I try to offer some comfort. "You know, David, this is an investigation, and I'm not at liberty to share this information with you. But I do want you to know that because of you, I believe I got what I came for. You have been instrumental in securing this evidence."

"Really? Wow! My friends will never believe any of this. What crime are you investigating?"

I hate to burst his bubble. "I can't tell you, and David, here's the hard part: it's extremely important that you not tell anyone I was here or what I was looking for. There's a chance the criminal still lives in the area, and if he finds out that I'm snooping around, I could lose him for good. I know you want to tell your buddies, but now is not the time." The look on his face says so much, but he's a trooper.

"I understand, I really do. I hope you find him. Will you let me know when I can tell, though?" He looks at me eagerly.

"You'll be the second one to know" — after my mother.

David fades from my visions and thoughts. Digging through the musty, dusty boxes this time, looking only at the customer names, I never come across another charge in 1983 or from either 1982 or 1984 to the Johnson family except for a Phillips screwdriver and some brass upholstery tacks. Cyrus doesn't appear to have a shoe fetish; he just needed two pairs of work boots in one year.

On my way back home with the invoices safely tucked into my notebook, I recognize that all I have is still only circumstantial evidence. As David had told me, there would be no record from a cash customer. For all I know, an outsider could have bought this particular brand of boots in Minnesota. But what is becoming clear is that Cyrus may have had more than dirt on his boots.

## CHAPTER VIII

I update my running journal on all my investigations with commentary on what I believe it all means, but I realize that nothing I have found can definitively lead me to where I want to be. Funny thing is, I don't know where I want to be. All I've believed about myself seems less important now. All that I thought I knew of my mother and her mother before her seems wrong now, as though my family history were more veneer than substance. I wonder, too, if that is true of me, if I am merely the antithesis of what my mother wanted me to be, a response to her and not an individual, separate from her. And if that is true, am I merely trying to prove my worth to her as this thing I've become? Or if I am wrong, am I simply trying to justify what I have become by completing what seems to be my life's work? As if I were still tied to the womb, the phone rings — my mother, according to the caller ID. I choose not to answer it. All that drives me is my need to satisfy this longing for the truth, which may not be a longing at all, but rather a drive to find something else: my grandmother, her ghost, or, as I tell myself, her killer. Cyrus, it seems, committed the crime, but all I have to go on is innuendo.

I must face this yearning, this something drawing me to find the truth. Whatever it is, it beckons me, and I can't keep up with it while running back and forth to work. Before I take a shower or have breakfast, I'm at the PD, waiting for the chief. He's not far behind me.

"Chief, you got a minute?" I ask tentatively. I've

always respected him but have had few dealings with him directly. I can tell he's surprised to see me.

"Sure, Kathleen. Come on back." Chief Canning is a tall white-haired man, younger than he appears. I follow him to the office.

"Chief, I've got a personal matter to take care of. It's nothing bad, really, but I've got to deal with it. I need maybe a couple of weeks off. I know it's short notice and all, but I do have the time coming, and I wouldn't ask if it weren't really important to me, to my family." I realize I'm babbling, but I can't help it. I feel guilty even though I'm telling him the truth. I know I'll put out other people, other officers, especially Joe, and I don't like it, but I've got to face things now, figure things out while I have the chance.

His eyes narrow slightly, more out of concern than anger. "If you need the time, I'll find it. Is there anything I can do for you, Kathleen? My door's always open to you, you know." He takes a fatherly tone with me.

"I appreciate it, Chief, but it's something I've got to do alone. It'll be fine, though—I promise." I'm hesitant to tell him more, and I don't know why.

The chief dismisses me, and I'm on my own, off to finish what I have started. I regret walking out as soon as I hit the threshold.

I am reluctant to take the money my grandmother hid, but Mother told me to keep it, and I vowed long ago not to touch my savings. Grandma's money should be enough to keep me in a motel and pay my expenses for a while, and she would understand, even be happy, I think, for me to use it, especially in this way. I call my parents but get no answer, so I leave a message that if they need me in the next few days, they can call me on my cell phone. We don't chat that often—partly my fault—and no doubt Mother would try to discourage me from following up on my quest. She's never expressed worry at my being in harm's way as a cop, but only at how it would appear. I imagine she might find it embarrassing that the granddaughter and not the mother chose to try and bring closure to the murder. Interesting, but I must make my plans. I pack a suitcase with clothes, toiletries, my notebook minus the pages already filled stuffed in my secret drawer, pepper spray, my off-duty weapon, and handcuffs. I always keep my badge in my wallet. I lock up and head back to the car, filled with some amount of anxiety, I believe, because I know I will learn the truth. I don't know why it is that I know it, but I feel that this is it, the moment I will prove myself to someone and, more specifically, to one of the three women of my family: my grandmother who I feel watches me, my mother who watches others, or me, who watches everyone. We will all learn the truth about the murder, and we will all know the truth about me, that although I have not followed in the footsteps outlined for me, I am still capable of making my own place. And I will be successful there. Grandma knows that. I think I know that.

The drive to Ellyson is more dramatic this time. I feel that something will be accomplished, that I will learn, without a doubt, who killed my grandmother. I have not yet made the rank of investigator, working more reactively to the present than contemplatively about the past. Investigation is a role I've yearned for, but I recognize that I still lack the requisite experience needed to attain it. Perhaps this will mark the dividing line.

I head directly to the Ellyson Motel, the only

overnight lodging in the area, to my knowledge anyway. It lies just off the highway west of town and is sparsely occupied, if the number of cars in the parking lot is any indication.

The desk clerk looks up at me from behind tortoiseshell glasses, and his narrow nose lifts up from the book he is reading. "Can I help you?" His accent, or rather the lack thereof, suggests he's not from this neck of the woods.

"Yes. I need a room, maybe for as long as two weeks." I imagine that this establishment doesn't often get long-term guests, but my request doesn't seem to faze him.

"Please fill out this form. How will you be paying for the room?" His eyes meet mine.

"Cash, I suppose. How much is it a night?"

"I can give you the weekly rate of forty-five dollars per night. That includes daily housekeeping service, cable TV, and all local calls are free."

"Sounds fine. If it's okay, I'll just pay for the first week now and see how my work goes." He gives me a week's total and the room key to my temporary home.

Surprisingly, the room is more spacious and brighter than I expected. I see no mildew in the bathtub in contrast to that vision of Grandma's decaying house with its rusted tub, still too alive in my memory. The carpet is mildly worn, but otherwise the room is quite pleasant. I take this all as a good sign, a sign that I'm doing what I should, and I feel a joy that I can't readily describe. I unpack the few items I brought from home along with my war-torn notebook to log my suspicions and findings. The overhead light highlights the stark whiteness of the page, and I am pushed to cover it with ink. I pull out my favorite fine-tip black pen and write across the top of this page, "CYRUS." On this trip I expect to prove him guilty of my grandmother's murder.

Because the *Ellyson Gazette* proved so helpful before, I decide to begin there again. This time, however, I'm looking for something about Cyrus. On the short drive here, I realized that he may have merited a mention in his mother's obituary. I calculate that she must have died in 1997.

Bea remembers me. "Well, hey, there, young thing. Still trying to find out about your roots, are you? What can I help you with today?" They aren't this friendly anywhere in Jackson.

"Nice to see you, Bea. As a matter of fact, I'm only going back to 1997. I think my grandfather's sister, Gracie, died that year." I look straight at her for a reaction, and I am not disappointed.

"Sounds about right," she says, but this time without a friendly, smiling face. "I'll get the microfilm." Bea steps off toward the spools while I consider picking her brain about this family. I decide to hold off, however, until I learn more.

I quickly come across Gracie's obituary in the March 1 issue of that year:

> *Gracie Johnson, long-time resident of Ellyson, died Tuesday evening in her home. She had been suffering with cancer for over two years, and according to her son Cyrus, she died in peace with him at her side.*

I almost overlook the picture inset into the column, however: of Cyrus and Gracie together. What shocks me, though, is that I know this man. He is the guard from the courthouse, the only less-than-hospitable person I've run across in the town. Neither Gracie nor Cyrus is smiling. Had I never known them or anything about them, what would still strike me about these two is the darkness of their faces, not in color, but in feeling. Although they stand side by side, they do not touch. Gracie leans heavily on a cane. Cyrus stands at least a foot taller, and even though he is much younger in this picture, little seems to have changed except for more pronounced wrinkles around his mouth, as if he frowns even in his sleep.

I quickly rewind the film while Bea wanders toward me. "Found what you're looking for, I'll bet. Seems everything begins and ends with family." I can only nod and walk out without a word. Bea's words reverberate. Everything does begin and end with family.

## CHAPTER IX

I have to question what I know. Life does begin with family, but it doesn't have to end that way, too. I am a granddaughter, but am I if my grandparents no longer exist? I am a daughter, but we dropped the pretense of the parent-child relationship long ago. I am a cop; there's nothing to question there, although I feel like I am less than one now because I'm out of my element, away from my turf, doing something I've never done before. I can see, however, as I write on this pad, that I am little more than an extension of my family, either attracted to them or repelled. I judge myself in relation to them, not to myself. Rather than absorbing all I see and creating the person I choose for myself, I am either reflecting or deflecting what they are, as if I were a mirrored surface. I write "GUILTY" at the bottom of the page, drop my pen, and head for the shower.

The hot water cascades down, pelts me with stinging tentacles that seem to pierce deep into me. GUILTY of judging my mother. GUILTY of false pride and elevated ego. GUILTY of an independence that has kept me separated from so many. Only in sleep can I escape these demons. I feel only the coolness of the sheets.

The high-pitched ring of the telephone rouses me. I choose not to answer it, preferring to examine a dream I can't recall, a dream that has left me sweaty and chilled and wondering. The sun has yet to set, but the neon red of the bedside clock suggests that the warmth of the day will soon fall away.

In these shadows between dusk and night, I remember the vision of the unpainted steeple in Ellyson which will soon be soaked with moonlight. It will be transfigured not by man but by nature, each degree of setting sun hiding more of its flaws yet still revealing the strength of its foundation. The other church, across the square, seems bent on hiding its flaws, too. It is not immune from that light that bares its imperfections, which appear to be more numerous than its cousin's. Which one am I?

My family has hidden long enough. I am going to face Cyrus, on my terms, in my way. I throw on my jeans and a T-shirt, grab my gun, badge, and even my notebook.

It's hard to be quiet when you have to. You try to stand noiselessly, but it only makes your heart beat louder, your breathing more labored. You feel the sweat rolling down your cheek onto your shirt in this expanse of humidity in the swamp, but you can't wipe it away. I have come alone, looking for Cyrus. At nearly dusk, I approach his home in Ellyson. I know what I'm doing is dangerous, but I want to understand what can't be understood: family in the form of a monster. I want my mother to know the truth, even if she can't face it. I want to look him in the eye. I want to solve the crime, be an investigator. My thoughts are complete, here in black and white, and I believe that my search is about to come to its end.

The house is an older clapboard house adjacent to a swamp. No one answers her knocks at the front door, but Kathleen sees a light not too far off, swinging back and forth among the trees, and approaches it, slowly but determined. She doesn't know for sure that Cyrus is the person she follows, but feels that he is. As she nears him, Kathleen confirms that the face on this man is indeed that of the guard from the courthouse, the man she identified as Cyrus from a newspaper clipping about his mother's death.

Kathleen yells to him, "Cyrus, can I talk to you for a minute?" He gives her no response. "Cyrus, I just need to ask you one question. Then I'll leave you alone, okay?"

"What do you want?" he sneers at her.

"Do you remember my grandmother, Emma Johnson?"

"Yes, what about her?" he responds as he takes a step toward her.

"Do you know how she died?" Kathleen doesn't move back. She doesn't know how.

"Yes, what about it?" He is only a couple of feet away now.

"Did you do it?" She steps toward him. She sees the darkness, but Kathleen refuses to let Cyrus see her fear.

"Yes."

"Why?" Kathleen asks, barely able to say the word. Her hand slowly reaches behind her, for the gun wedged in her waistband.

"She wouldn't sell her land to Mama, but we knew Otis's daughter would. She never cared much about the country. They said there'd be oil around here, lots of it." Cyrus clenches his fists in anger.

"But they didn't find any. You killed her for nothing." Knowing she was right didn't make the truth any easier for Kathleen to hear.

"We ain't never had good luck. Nothing but bad. And you're gonna know just how that feels.

Kathleen has the answer, but she has no backup. Joe told her always to wait for backup.

# PART II

## CHAPTER I

Joe Carpenter drove up to the station, not surprised to see Chris Myer's patrol car there. He'd been working together with Joe for over a week, a retired officer just filling in for Kathleen. Chris was a by-the-book cop who enjoyed reading and then rereading the Florida statutes more than working the streets. He drove Joe crazy. He could cite most of the esoteric laws chapter and verse, but he had difficulty enforcing any of them. Joe knew the law, too, but his knowledge focused on the more often used laws Joe tried to keep his distance.

"How you doing, Joe?" Chris asked, unaware of Joe's disdain for him.

"Fine. Where's the pass-down sheet, Wendy?" Joe walked past Chris into the dispatcher's room.

"Right here, grouchy." Wendy knew why Joe felt the way he did.

"Any word about that damned Kathleen?" Joe stared down at the pages, not registering what he saw.

"Nothing. Nothing at all." Wendy knew that the chief was growing impatient with Kathleen's absence. He had to pay for another officer, and when Chris wasn't available, he had to pay someone else overtime. Her adventure was growing costly. Joe was just as upset with Kathleen, more so, really, but for a very different reason. She hadn't bothered to tell him what was going on in her life, something so dramatic that it took her away from her work, her work with him. Even from three feet away, Wendy could feel the anger radiate from him.

Joe made a few cursory notes about the day's events, grabbed an 800 radio, and walked out without a word to Chris. Chris didn't take it personally. He didn't take it at all. He was oblivious.

Not only was Joe furious that Kathleen had taken off without telling him, but he was also astonished that she hadn't been in touch since. They had talked about a lot of things in the time they had known each other, and he had held nothing back. Now he knew that she had.

But he had little time to consider where she might be, or with whom. Wendy radioed out a call. "We have a disturbance at the hospital with a signal twelve, possibly intoxicated."

*We're not police; we're bouncers,* thought Joe to himself. "Ten-four. ETA five."

Joe was disappointed to hear that Chris was en route, too. Atlas broke from his slumber when he sensed the accelerator nearing the floorboard. Once they were parked outside the ambulance bay, he quieted down.

The police were always conscientious about taking care of the medical profession. The argument ran that there may come a day when the police really needed them, so they were sure to be there for the doctors and nurses who called for help.

The side doors automatically swung open for Joe, and the pointing fingers told him where to go, not that Joe needed any directional hints—he could hear the shouting.

The screamer was alone in his room, yelling for pain medication. Joe stood in the doorway to assess the situation. "Hey, man. What's the problem? These people are trying to help you, and you're making it hard on them." Joe noted that the patient was bleeding over his left eye, and his nose looked as though it might be broken.

"Shit. They called the damned *po*-lice." Joe hated it when people called him that, with the accent on the "po." He stared at Joe.

"If you don't want their help, get the hell out of here and make room for someone who does." If there was one thing that Joe really couldn't stand, it was a drunk. When he was in high school, his next-door neighbor was always drunk. And loud. And obnoxious. Many nights Joe lay in bed listening to the ranting of this man at all hours of the night.

"I do want help, man. They were just hurting me, that's all." The guy was beginning to look deflated, as though the alcohol was slowing his brain down. Or perhaps he didn't want to push the *po*-lice too far.

"I'll get them in here because you need the help, but if you raise your voice or a fist, I'm tossing your ass out on the sidewalk. Got it?" Joe noticed Chris standing behind him.

"Yes, sir. I won't do them no harm." And with that, he lay down quietly. The radiologist took X-rays of his face and found a fracture just below the bridge of his nose. All they could do for it was ice it down until the swelling slowed. His face had begun to contort from the inflammation. A nurse sutured the cut over his eye.

"Who did this to you?" Joe asked, looking for someone to bust.

"No one. I just tripped." They both knew it was a lie, but there was nothing Joe could do if the man wouldn't tell him the truth. He told Chris to stay until the guy was released, just in case he got out of control again. Chris didn't look too happy, but he wouldn't dare question authority. By the book.

Joe had some peace to consider what to do about

Kathleen. He tried her cell phone again. For the forty-somethingth time. But on the second ring, someone answered.

It was a man's voice. *Damn it to hell,* Joe said to himself, *if she's been off with some guy, I will never speak to her again.*

"Hello?" said the mystery man.

"Who the hell is this?" replied Joe, not able to control himself.

"This is Deputy Billy Anderson with the Ellyson County Sheriff's Office. Who the hell are *you*?"

Joe's heart pumped louder, filling him with a sudden, sickening sense. "Sorry, man. This is Joe Carpenter with the Jackson Police Department. This is my partner's cell phone, Kathleen Whibbs. Where is Kathleen? You surely must know, right?" Joe knew it sounded as though he were pleading, but he feared that even if he could get an explanation, it wasn't going to be good.

"We just found her cell phone. Do you have a number for her parents? We need to reach them. She's not married, is she? I noticed when I met her she wasn't wearing a ring."

"No. She's not married. You've got to tell me. I'm a cop. I work with her—every night. You've got to tell me. Is she okay?" His hand was shaking the phone against his ear.

"You know I shouldn't tell you anything. But she's not dead, at least not that we know. Now, get me that number, all right?"

Joe got the number for the Ellyson County Sheriff's Office and gave Billy his own contact numbers, along with his police chief's name. Joe didn't know Kathleen's parents' number, so he radioed Wendy to find out the information. He resisted all her pleadings about why he needed to know. "I'll tell you when I make it back to the station. Give all the calls to Chris, okay, Wendy? I'm coming up to the PD."

"All right, Joe, but you've *got* to tell me what's going on."

But Joe didn't have a clue what was going on. All he knew was that Kathleen was possibly alive, though even that was uncertain and a stranger held her cell phone. He had never stopped to think that she could be in danger. Joe was fearful. He could now feel the weight of the unknown growing in his stomach.

Wendy knew something was very wrong when she saw the pallor of Joe's skin. He could barely speak the words he needed to say. Not even faced with a gun at point-blank range had Joe known such fear.

"Did you get it?" he finally asked as he sat down in the only empty chair.

"No. It's in her personnel file, and I don't have a key. The chief's on his way."

Wendy stared at him, trying to get a read on how serious the situation was. "Is Kathleen okay?" She really cared about her. Kathleen had never thought twice about helping Wendy out when she needed it. Anytime she went to grab a bite to eat, she would always ask if she could pick something up for Wendy. And Kathleen would never take a dime in return.

"I don't know. But I do know something's wrong—I just don't know how wrong yet." They both sat in silence until the chief walked in.

"What the hell is going on with Kathleen? What did you find out, Joe?" The chief stood in the threshold, frozen, while Joe explained what he knew. The chief took the number for the Ellyson County Sheriff's Office and promised to find out more.

Joe couldn't stand the waiting. He walked down the hallway toward the chief's office but found the door closed. He paced. He wondered. He didn't know why Kathleen was in Alabama. At a complete loss, he approached the chief's door, hoping to eavesdrop. The door swung open just as he began to lean close.

"The doors are too heavy for that," said the chief. "I know—I've tried." Joe made no apology.

"Seems they found her car with her cell phone in it yesterday. It was abandoned near some woods. Looked like someone tried to set it on fire, but for some reason the fire burned out. They wanted to know why she was there this time. I told them I didn't know, but I thought it had to do with family. They're calling her parents now."

"This time? When was the last time? Anything that can tell us anything?" Joe had bounced back from concerned friend to eager cop.

"I don't know when she was there before although she called in one day saying she was out of town and couldn't make it in to work. I had to get a reserve officer to cover her shift. They found out she was registered at a motel in town, but they've already tried to call her room. No answer." The chief could sense a change in Joe's attitude. "Now, don't you get any ideas about going there. I need you here, Joe. But I told them if they needed our help, we'd come on over. Let's see what they find at the motel first. Then we can decide what to do."

Joe knew already. He was leaving. Something had gone very wrong. He wasn't there for her—she didn't have her backup.

## CHAPTER II

Gut instinct has always served Joe well. His gut told him to go, despite the chief's order not to, so he prepared to leave for a place he'd never been. The chief knew he couldn't hold Joe back, and but for making sure that all the shifts were covered, he'd be on his way, too. Sometimes leadership got in the way of friendship. But in spite of what the chief had told Joe, he trusted Joe to do what was necessary and what was right.

Joe had never been to Ellyson, but he knew which roads led there. He changed into his civilian clothes, swapped his patrol car for his Jeep, and headed out. It was nearly ten, just after his shift, when he set off. There was no moon.

As he neared the town, Joe was acutely aware of just how small a small town could be. But for its compact epicenter, there was little else to Ellyson. Joe noted that just over two hours had passed since his call to Kathleen's cell phone was answered. He was both hopeful and apprehensive when he drove up to the sheriff's office, quite easy to spot with three squad cars parked in front.

"Evening, or maybe good morning. I'm Joe Carpenter. I work with Kathleen Whibbs at the Jackson Police Department. I had to come, you know. Did you find her yet?" His initial scan around the room did not find her there.

"I'm Sheriff West. I wish we had good news. Can't find hide nor hair of her here. Any idea what she might be doing back here?" The sheriff appeared worried.

"None at all, Sheriff. I never knew she was here in the first place. Where's her car? Has crime scene taken a look at it?" As the words left his mouth, he realized how foolish he sounded. A small department would never have crime scene investigators.

The sheriff wasn't bothered. "We had it towed down to Mitty's Garage. We've dusted it for prints, but we've requested the Alabama State Police's forensic team to have a look. They'll be here by breakfast. 'Course, we've checked her grandmother's place, but there's no sign of her there." Sheriff West thought he noticed a confused look on Joe's face.

"Grandmother's place. Kathleen has family here?" He sat down, overcome by the sudden realization that he knew so little about someone he knew so much about.

As the sheriff filled Joe in on the details of the murder and Kathleen's subsequent visit to town, Joe started to feel that pit-of-the-stomach lump again. *Why didn't you let me help you, Kathleen?* he thought to himself. She was searching for the killer; he would bet his badge on it. His daydreaming was interrupted by a phone call.

"Calm down. Now, Jack, you know there's nothing we can do about it. Well, we're a little busy right now, so when we get a chance, we'll check it out, all right? Go to sleep—you won't hear it then." He shook his head as he hung up the phone. "Cyrus's dog's howling in the shack. Jack says he hasn't seen ol' Cyrus for days. Poor hound dog's probably run out of food. Say, Billy, on your way home, check it out, would you? Probably nothing."

"Sheriff, you want me to go now?" Billy didn't want to miss any action. This was the most excitement he'd had in years, not that he was happy about the circumstances.

"Yeah, I'll call you if anything breaks. Probably not much will happen until morning, anyway."

Billy grudgingly walked out. He never liked to leave things unfinished. But he didn't yet know he would be the one to close the book on Kathleen.

## CHAPTER III

People didn't just disappear in Ellyson, at least not visitors. The older generation was dying off pretty regularly, but that didn't count. But pretty cops visiting town didn't disappear. Billy couldn't accept what was starting to shape up as the truth.

His patrol car headlights illuminated the darkness that surrounded the house, more like a shack than a house, really. One light was on inside. Billy rolled his window down. Sure enough, Cyrus's dog was having a fit. No owner and no car probably meant no food. He approached the house holding his flashlight and tested the back door. It was unlocked.

"Cyrus, you in here? Cyrus?" A black-and-tan coon hound met him at the back door, practically knocking him down. "Come back, Pete. Here boy." Pete ran off into the swamp.

"Damn it. Instead of looking for a lady, I'm off chasing a dog. Same old story." He set off in the dog's direction. Suddenly, Pete stopped running, and Billy was hopeful that the mutt had gotten the vinegar out of his body. "Here, Pete. Here, boy." But instead of coming to him, Pete once again began to howl. "Stupid dog, come here!" As he approached Pete, Billy noticed something in the beam of his flashlight at the dog's feet.

"What is it, boy? A shirt? Jeans? Hell no – it's a body."

## CHAPTER IV

As soon as the call came over the air, two patrol cars and one Jeep rolled out from the sheriff's office. Lights and sirens. Accelerator to the floorboard. Wide open. Joe brought up the rear because he didn't know where he was going. He was following blindly, numbly, mutely, except for the occasional "God, no, please, God. No."

Billy was unwinding the seldom used roll of crime scene tape. He wasn't quite sure where it should begin and end, so he started at the house and moved from there to the swamp. He got dizzy wrapping the tape around the slender trees. He'd never seen anything like it before — not that it was horrifying, or even messy. Just a clean gunshot right to the chest. The blood looked like wet tar, not bright red or even crimson. Black. Too damn black. He tried to feel for a pulse, but he knew already. She had been dead for a while — a long while.

He led the speechless crowd of sheriff, two fellow deputies, and one distraught police officer to his find. The brightness of the flashlights shining together shielded their faces from one another, and each man, in his own way, was happy for it. The sheriff made the identification clear to the rest of the procession. "Damn it, Kathleen. Who the hell did this to you?" He shook his head, not in disgust but in disbelief. No one had been murdered in his jurisdiction for more years than he could remember. All eyes turned to Joe, and then away.

Joe stood over her limp body and stared. He

considered all they had been through together, and pleaded for God to show him why he hadn't shared in this, too. Joe bent down and drew back some wisps of hair that had fallen across her brow. When he realized they were stiff, too, he drew back and found a tree where he could expel all that he felt. Her hair was still, even in the breeze, as was her body, her smile, her heart, her brain, her laughter.

Once he could breathe again, Joe called the PD on his cell phone. Deborah, the overweight and underworked dispatcher, answered. "Get the chief to call me on my cell." He was curt, but he wasn't thinking straight, and he really didn't care anyway.

"Well, I'm not going to bother the chief at one in the morning without a very good reason. Why do you need the chief?" She was clearly annoyed, even though she had heard rumblings of concern about Kathleen's whereabouts when she came on duty.

"Call him now, or I swear to God..." He held his tongue. "Just call him and never mind a reason. He *knows* what it's about." And he hung up. Within a minute, his phone rang. It was the chief. Through muffled sobs, Joe told him what they'd found, and asked him to send a crime scene unit out.

"Is the sheriff there, Joe? I've got to talk to him first, you know. It's his part of the country." Joe handed over the phone and heard no more.

The sheriff soon handed him back the phone. "Joe, I appreciate all you're trying to do, but this is an Alabama crime, and I gotta use Alabama people. I've got the crime scene unit from the state police en route. I've got a K-9 unit coming, too. They'll do a good job, Joe. I promise. We will find out what happened. I promise, Joe."

Joe was out of words.

"Come on, Joe, help us out. Let's mark this scene off together. We've got to watch where we step. That's right, come on." Joe was following blindly again.

Crime scene didn't arrive for more than an hour, but time was meaningless to Joe. The chief did show up but immediately conferred with the sheriff about their findings. Joe sat motionless outside the perimeter.

He didn't notice the approach of footsteps. "Joe, they're doing all they can here. I've talked to everyone, and these are capable people. We couldn't do any better. They'll handle this right. But I've got to go back to Jackson. Come with me. After I take care of some things, let's go get some coffee and breakfast. We can't do anything here."

Joe refused to leave. "K-9 unit hasn't shown up yet. I want to see what they find. And anyway, Kathleen and I...well, we go together, damn it. I don't leave without her, Chief."

The chief knew he could say nothing more until then—until his officer was carried out in a black bag on a white stretcher. He'd never lost an officer, not this way. And he didn't know why he'd lost this one. He didn't know how he would explain this to her parents, but he had no choice.

"Joe, I have to go now. Stay with her. You're doing the right thing. Call me when you're done here. Do you want me to get Pat to drive over?" The chief really didn't know what to do for Joe, but he knew he had to let Kathleen's family know, and he would be the one to say the words.

"No, I'm okay. I'll call you." With that, Joe sat on the hood of his car and watched the crime scene lights dance among the trees.

The K-9 unit arrived with their German shepherd,

Marko. The handler established from the deputies where everyone had already walked, and armed with that information, cast Marko outside the established perimeter where he was sure no other officers had been. Joe was not surprised to learn that Marko was unable to pick up any scent indicating that the killer most likely left out the same way he had come in, and since that was already contaminated by the initially responding deputies, there was little the K-9 handler could do in getting a good track. The killer may have left in some kind of vehicle, but any tire tracks had been buried by Billy's patrol car.

Shortly after daybreak, after the state police packed up their findings, the medical examiners arrived. The two men spoke quietly to the sheriff before gathering their supplies and heading out under the yellow ribbon. Joe waited the hour and more that it took to remove Kathleen's body from the scene, and then he walked beside her stretcher the last few yards to the investigators' hearse, the civilian's death bed.

## CHAPTER V

The suspect was obvious: Cyrus. It was his land, and he was missing along with his truck. The motive was something else. No one even knew why Kathleen had been there. As far as the sheriff was concerned, she was just looking into the family's homestead, nothing more, nothing less. As far as Kathleen's chief was concerned, she was sorting out a personal matter having to do with "family," whatever that meant. Kathleen's mother knew she had been to Ellyson, but just to the house, to "face her past," whatever that was. And Joe seemed to know less than anyone. He had only recently learned of Ellyson, its broken-down houses, and a murdered grandmother. His shock and sadness quickly shifted into anger.

*Well, Kathleen, you didn't trust me with what was going on,* he reflected. *Well, fine. We were never that close, you know. You didn't pay attention to what I taught you, anyway. If you had, you wouldn't be where you are, and I wouldn't have seen your lifeless body in that hell hole. You weren't that great a cop.* He knew he was lying to himself, but at that moment it was all he could do. He didn't know what the truth was anymore—what *any* truth was. He didn't really even know the partner he thought he knew. He didn't understand how or why she let down her guard enough to get hurt—to get killed. He didn't think something like this could happen to someone he cared about. Joe recognized the irony that he, a cop, had never known anyone personally who had been shot, much less murdered. He had taken his first step into the personal darkness of police work, the darkness of life.

Joe reflected on Kathleen's fate as he numbly drove to her funeral a week after her body was discovered. The requisite autopsy showed she was killed with two shots, .40 caliber, one to the chest and the other to her neck, straight into the vocal chords, as though her murderer wanted her silenced. He was successful, of course, but Joe hoped the words she could no longer say would someday be heard in evidence or testimony. The scumbag even had the gall to use her own gun to do it.

Pat sat shotgun in the patrol car, but neither exchanged a word. Each man was lost in his own state of grieving, unable to share his thoughts or feelings — unwilling to communicate them. Sharing only made it real, and neither man could accept that yet. Joe fixated on the hearse three cars in front of them. He remembered a time he worked a funeral with Kathleen, just stopping traffic at lights so the procession could travel unimpeded toward the cemetery. Once the procession left the city limits, a deputy would then accompany the mourners to the location. Joe noticed at the time that Kathleen stood outside her car at the city line, straight and tall at parade rest as the cars passed. It wasn't a requirement of her department; it was something she required of herself.

Police funerals aren't that different from military funerals: lots of uniforms, military-style taps, bagpipes, ceremony. But there is one clear distinction: those who attend. Not only do family, friends and fellow officers come, but also officers from other departments who don't even know the dead. It's an unspoken rule within the police that if you have the off- time to do it, you will travel to another cop's funeral if you're from an adjacent agency, and occasionally when you're not. Kathleen's funeral was no different, the chief noted, except that the number of police officers and departments in attendance was greater than usual. Alabama was almost as well-represented as Florida, with officers from all over the state. Three cars from Miami even made the drive. Georgia, Louisiana, and Texas sent officers.

None of this was lost on Kathleen's mother. Losing her daughter, another woman of the family, to a violent death, was almost too much for Sarah. But something about all those cars and officers, the sheer number of people who cared about her daughter enough to show up, brought her comfort, coupled, of course, with regret. She began to understand how well loved her daughter was despite her occupation, maybe even because of it. She realized also that Kathleen's job brought with it another family, complete with relatives from all over the country, who for some reason, wanted to make the trek to tell her good-bye, and they were there solely because of her occupation. For the first time in so long, Sarah Whibbs was proud of her daughter — proud of the life she led, the calling she followed — and yet unable to tell her. What had made Kathleen so independent? What had drawn her from a life of relative privilege to a life working with so many who had none? Sarah thought back to the kind of girl her daughter once was.

"Mom, I want to be a nurse when I grow up." Kathleen was nine or ten at the time.

"You do? Why is that?" she asked.

"Because I want to help people, of course," Kathleen replied, as though she had been asked the stupidest of questions.

*And how stupid of me,* Sarah thought to herself. Kathleen always cared about people, even when she was young. Once she donated all her summer earnings to a family who lost everything to a house fire. And when I asked her why she wanted to be a cop, she simply replied that she wanted to make her little piece of the world a better, safer place. *And I condemned her for it,* she said, almost out loud. *I'm proud of you, Kathleen. Damn it, I want you to know I am very proud of you.*

Joe suffered through the funeral in a different way. As one of the pallbearers, he had to keep face despite how he felt inside. Through tearful eyes no one could see behind dark sunglasses, he noticed the hundreds of uniforms, but not the faces that peered out from them. Joe couldn't make eye contact with anyone, even though Kathleen had taught him that was the only way to really know someone. He didn't want to know anyone. All he wanted was to carry her in the box that housed her, carefully and quietly, to the last place he would ever see her—the shiny white box with gold-colored handles, draped in red, white, and blue.

The casket landed noiselessly on the metal strapping above the grave. The Reverend John Turner, the family's spiritual leader for most of Kathleen's life, gave the eulogy. "It is difficult to come to terms with the death of someone so full of life," he said, looking out at the silent gathering. "Kathleen made not only her living but also her life about helping others. For those of you who knew her, you knew that Kathleen would do everything in her power to help you, or me, or a stranger, in any way she could. We may never know what happened that so senselessly brought about her death, but we will always remember Kathleen as a bright light when we were in darkness." The Reverend Turner went on to try to comfort Kathleen's family, but Joe could listen no more. He was lost again, back in Alabama, struggling to understand something he knew nothing about. Still unable to believe she was gone, he vowed then, over her grave while whispering beneath the minister's words, that he would find who did this and why, and send him or her straight to hell.

Joe's reflections abruptly halted with the first volley by the honor guard's firing detail. Never had he flinched at the report of a firearm before that moment. And he flinched three times, each time the seven rifles fired. "Ready...aim...fire!" he heard the commander instruct. But all he could see was Cyrus, standing over Kathleen's dying body, aiming to shoot her again. He broke out in a cold sweat. "Ready...aim...fire!"

Joe, as well as the other officers, steeled himself for the next stage of telling Kathleen goodbye: taps. The mournful notes moved both veteran and rookie to quiet tears. "Amazing Grace" followed on the bagpipes. At its conclusion, the honor guard carefully folded the flag covering the casket. Kathleen's mother remained stoic during the presentation of the stars and stripes, while her father wept openly.

The civilians were not prepared for the last element of police funeral protocol. Over the chief's patrol car's PA system, dispatch gave a farewell radio announcement. "Jackson to unit seventeen...Jackson to unit seventeen...Jackson to unit seventeen...Attention, all units. Officer Kathleen Whibbs is ten-seven from service. May she rest in peace."

*I will never rest in peace,* Joe thought to himself. After the service, he dropped Pat off and drove home alone, stopping to talk to no one.

Sending the murderer to hell, however, posed a great challenge. No weapon had been recovered, although it was determined that Kathleen's gun had been used. No recoverable trace evidence was located at the scene. All the police had to work with was a dead body, her abandoned car, and a missing homeowner. A BOLO went out for Cyrus's truck, but so far it had not been spotted. There wasn't much to work with, but Joe was driven to do what he could. His first step the next day was to call Kathleen's family.

"Mrs. Whibbs, this is Joe Carpenter. How are you holding up?" Joe had misgivings about bothering her. They had only met twice, and they had spoken little. But things were different now.

"Okay, Joe. I just can't believe it still. I just can't believe it." Her voice was weak.

"I know. I can't, either. And I really hate to ask you this now, but I just have to." Joe sat down on his couch, weak from the conversation.

"What is it?"

"I'm going to find her killer. I swear to you that I am. But I have to understand why she was there. She didn't tell me anything." Joe hoped to learn more than he had from the sheriff. He remembered to breathe.

Mrs. Whibbs explained in a tearful monotone about her mother's murder so long ago, in much the same way that the sheriff had told him—about the abandoned house and Kathleen's desire to do something about it. She did not divulge anything about the money or the journal. She added that Cyrus was a relative, which Joe already knew from the police in Ellyson.

"Cyrus's mother was not close with our family. She didn't care much for my mother. But Cyrus—we had nothing to do with the man. Why, I doubt I would even know him if I saw him. I can't imagine why he would want to hurt his own flesh and blood." She tried to regain her lost composure.

"Do you have the keys to the house there? I'd like to retrace her steps and see if they can tell me something."

"Kathleen took them. She must have them." She said the words before she thought. Joe heard her gasp on the phone, and then the line went dead.

*Damn it.* He needed to drive back to Ellyson, felt he had no choice. And he only had twenty-four hours in which to do it. He was expected at work the next day. He changed into jeans from his uniform, starched stiff for the funeral, and set off for Alabama. He didn't think to call Jennifer as he left.

Since Kathleen had disappeared from Joe's life, he had thought little of Jennifer. As he drove toward Ellyson, he pondered why his feelings should wane. He loved Jennifer—he was sure of that—but they didn't share the same passions that he had with Kathleen. He admitted to himself that he had looked out for Kathleen both on and off duty. But then, Kathleen had done the same for him. Not that Jennifer hadn't, but it was just in a different way. It was a bond between police officers, a bond no outsider could really understand. He loved Kathleen as a best friend, and he prayed that somehow she died knowing how much he cared. Joe felt certain that Jennifer understood his need to find Kathleen's killer, that she would support him and his effort, and that she would never begrudge the relationship he and Kathleen once had. He had to focus now, and Jennifer would know that.

His first stop was the sheriff's office. Sheriff West and Billy, along with some suits, were crowded into the small office. Joe worked very hard to stay calm, not ask what the hell everyone was doing sitting around the office. Not demand that they get busy doing something. Not suggest that he take over the investigation. Sheriff West sensed some of this.

"Slow down, there, Joe. We're following up on some things and just waiting for a call back. This is our number one priority. Don't you worry about it. We'll find out what happened." Joe noticed the dark circles under the sheriff's eyes. He forced himself to calm down. In the past week since finding Kathleen's body, Joe had done little more than phone Billy or whoever answered to see if they found Cyrus's truck or if Kathleen's car had given them any meaningful evidence. Joe spent most of his time on the couch, sleeping with nightmares.

The sheriff interrupted his thoughts. "The state police did find something in her car that gives us some clues," he said. "One of the investigators found a notebook Kathleen stuffed under her seat. I'll let you look at a copy of it. It's partially burned from the fire, but most of it's legible." The sheriff pulled a photocopied set of documents from his desk and handed it to Joe. No one spoke as he read the words, and Joe said nothing once he finished. He now understood.

"Do you have the keys to the Johnsons' house? I just want to see what Kathleen saw. Maybe it could tell us something." He said "us," but he meant "me."

"We've inventoried Kathleen's belongings, but we found no keys, Joe. I can only guess that those house keys were on her keychain, which wasn't found in the car. But you've got a good point. We've been by there and walked through it, but didn't find anything. Anyway, why don't you and Billy go 'round to the Johnson house and just take a look? Couldn't hurt. We've got the Johnsons' permission to enter the house as we see fit." Billy seemed grateful to have a chance to do something other than wait. He jumped out of his chair and headed for the door.

"We'll take my car, if you don't mind. It's got all my gear in it." Billy didn't really have any gear other than what was strapped to his waist, but he really wanted to be in charge of something or someone, and Joe was just that person.

"I appreciate your indulging me here," Joe offered to the sheriff, a tacit apology for being difficult earlier.

Neither man uttered a word during the short drive to the house. Nothing seemed out of place as far as Billy was concerned, and nothing seemed *in* place to Joe. He had suddenly been thrust into a life he never dreamed existed. Billy tried the front door, but it was locked. The back door, however, was more welcoming. Nothing impeded their entrance into Kathleen's past. Joe instinctively drew his weapon, but with one glance from Billy, he returned it to its holster. Entering an unlocked structure almost always called for a drawn weapon in his world, but apparently not here in Billy's terrain. This home, this town, were not at all a part of a world Joe had ever known. They walked from room to empty room, not knowing the furniture layout, conversations, memories, arguments or mysteries that Kathleen had recently relived. Nothing here held any meaning to either of them or offered any answers. The rubber soles of Joe's boots squeaked across the floor as if they were wet. He didn't like the sound.

Discouraged, they left out the back door, which they wanted to lock but couldn't without the key. Joe didn't know where to go from there, so he returned to the sheriff's office with Billy, hoping he could learn more or that they had learned more. But he was disappointed there, too. Other than the usual questions about where Cyrus could be, there was little conversation of interest. The sheriff had spoken to Cyrus's supervisor at the courthouse who had heard nothing at all from the man. He did, however, give the sheriff Cyrus's identification picture, and the sheriff distributed it all over the county as well as in the western part of Florida. No one knew of any friends or family that Cyrus would turn to. He had no credit cards; there was no trail to follow. The BOLO was out there, and on that they had pinned all hope.

Joe returned to Florida demoralized, not only by life's twists but also by what he perceived to be a diminishing ability to read people and situations, an ability that had once served him well. He should have known something was up with Kathleen. *I should have seen something and didn't. I missed it. How could I ever be a good cop? Have I ever really been one?* He began to question even the things he knew.

No answers ever emerge from despair, he realized, so at a convenience store near his apartment, he bought a six-pack of beer, the second such purchase of his life. The first was a week ago. He hated the taste, but there was something cathartic about discomfort right now, and the diffusion of pain was what Joe sought—to match the pain within to the pain on the outside. He drank until body and soul reached equilibrium. And then he slept.

## CHAPTER VI

The realization of Kathleen's impact on the world around her remained with her mother during her mourning. Mrs. Whibbs wondered, if it had been she who died, would so many have cared? She considered that her own mother's funeral had been much the same, filled with people she never knew, who came from all over and then again, nowhere, to pay their respects and whisper their good-byes. *No,* she thought, *it will be different for me.*

Andrew Whibbs was taken aback by his wife's strength. His mourning consumed him, and perhaps Sarah sensed that, because she asked little of him. He couldn't pass through the threshold of his daughter's apartment, nor could he even drive in her neighborhood. His pain was too raw.

Although she had never used it, Sarah knew exactly where she kept Kathleen's extra apartment key — something she needed now. The Alabama State Police wanted to search her apartment for anything telling. They hoped to find information that might divulge to them more about why she had been in Ellyson, and specifically why she was looking for Cyrus. Sarah was prepared to go at their request but not without an ally. She thought Joe would want to be there and help, so she got his number from the police department and called him at home.

"Morning, Joe. I hope I haven't called too early."

It took Joe a moment to wake from his beer haze. "No, Mrs. Whibbs. Have they found out something? Did they find him? His car?"

She cut off the litany. "No, nothing like that. It's just that I need to go to her apartment to let in the state police, and I thought you might want to be there." Joe was pleased to know they were doing their job.

"Sure, what time?" He was wide awake now.

"At nine. Can you make it?"

"I'll be there, Mrs. Whibbs. No problem."

It was nearly eight, so Joe jumped into the shower, gulped some coffee and microwaved a slice of cold pizza. He felt better than he had in more than a week, because he was actually doing something proactive—at least he hoped so. But then it occurred to him that he would be in Kathleen's place without Kathleen. That had never happened. He would see her family pictures on the table, her neat and tidy rooms, her often-empty refrigerator. Joe began to dread going. But he couldn't say no, not now, and just maybe he would learn something that would help him find her killer.

He arrived early and stayed in his parked car, engine off, radio off, listening to the silence, occasionally punctuated by some door opening or closing nearby. He had never noticed how immaculate the apartment complex was. It had been around for ten years or more, but the paint looked fresh; the wooden facade was the soft color of butter. The contrast against the pale green shutters felt pleasing. Jasmine bushes surrounded the walkways highlighting the distinct boundary between the natural and the artificial.

The police arrived next, and before Joe could get out of his car, Mrs. Whibbs drove up.

"Hello. I'm Kathleen's mother, Sarah. I appreciate all you're doing," she assured the police. Joe was ashamed of his own weakness in the face of Sarah's strength. "Hi, Joe. Thanks so much for coming. My husband couldn't make it." She proceeded directly to the door and opened its lock, half expecting someone to emerge from the doorway.

The police investigator spoke for the first time. "Mrs. Whibbs, we're going to need to go through all her things. We don't know what we're looking for, or even if there's something here that might help us. Would you rather wait outside?" Joe couldn't tell if he asked out of concern for her or just to keep her out of their way.

"I'll be fine...I think. You go right in and do what you need to, but I'm coming in, too." And in she marched. Joe entered next, and the police followed.

Joe felt as though he were one of the criminals he fought so hard to find. He didn't belong here, not without Kathleen, and he had difficulty moving from the doorway. What drew him in finally was a photograph on the kitchen counter of the two of them. Jennifer had taken it a couple of months ago. He had the other copy, but his wasn't in a frame. Instinctively he wiped off the accumulated dust with the hem of his T-shirt. Kathleen would not like that. She kept her things clean and neat.

The police worked slowly and systematically, opening every orifice of every piece of furniture, every drawer, every stored purse, every bottle in the medicine cabinet, checking every pocket of every article of clothing hanging in her closet. They reviewed bank statements, looked through old invoices, even went through her e-mail. Nothing told them anything about Cyrus or Ellyson. Nothing told them much about Kathleen Whibbs, either. From the contents of her home, they could tell two things: she loved police work and she loved to read. There was very little of sentimental value other than photographs and a few cards amassed over the years from men of whom Mrs. Whibbs and Joe knew very little. Somewhat embarrassed by the paucity of information they retrieved the state police officers politely bowed out. Mrs. Whibbs nodded and turned to Joe.

"Joe, could you stay a little longer? I want to ask you a few things."

During the two-hour search, Joe often checked Mrs. Whibbs's face for signs of suffering and distress. He certainly saw sadness, but she was not overcome. She was tough, he thought, just like her daughter.

"Sure, I've got a little more time." Joe, on the other hand, knew he was weak.

"I don't know what to do with Kathleen's things. There are no siblings who could use her belongings, and as far as I know, you are—you were, that is—her closest friend."

Joe saw her strength begin to chip away. "Anyway, I'll give her clothes to the needy, but her kitchen table and chest of drawers...well, could you use them? The other pieces aren't likely something you would want." She was beginning to lose her composure. Joe had not expected anything like this. How could he accept? How could he not?

"I will think of her and remember her, and ...Mrs. Whibbs?" She could no longer hold back her grief.

Once her sadness was temporarily washed away, Mrs. Whibbs left Joe with an extra apartment key which she had made at a nearby hardware store. "I don't want to rush you, but I can't keep coming back here. Could you get the furniture out in the next couple of days? That way I can take care of the rest later this week, I hope."

"I'll do it. Thanks, Mrs. Whibbs. I don't know what to say, really."

"Sometimes words don't work, Joe. Good-bye."

Joe drove home with the windows down, radio

blasting out "Don't Stop Thinking About Tomorrow." He hated it when people drove around exuding noise pollution from their cars. *If I were a cop, I'd write myself a ticket,* he told himself. He couldn't help but smile, but only briefly.

## CHAPTER VII

Joe felt relieved to have Pat's company that afternoon on duty. They understood each other well enough to know that conversation was out of the question, and so they patrolled in silence, not really looking for anything in particular, but rather looking for nothing at all. Their self-imposed coma worked for a while, until the dispatcher roused them.

"Unit nine, got a report of a signal one driver heading east on Lakeview. Caller says he's just passing the EZ Mart at Yates. Says he's all over the road. Appears to be a late-model Ford Explorer, dark in color. Stand by for tag...Negative, unit nine. No tag information available."

"Ten-four, ten fifty-one." Saying the words didn't give Joe the old adrenaline rush that usually accompanied a call. He remained impassive. He hated DUI calls. The paperwork was always a nightmare, and it wasn't even dinnertime yet.

Joe turned north on Caroline Street to intercept Lakeview just east of Yates. Had he driven up five seconds later, he might have missed it. At least there was no doubt that this was the car — he couldn't maintain his lane. Pat flipped on the lights as Joe eased in behind the weaving car. Atlas immediately began to bark, sensing important work ahead.

"Unit nine, Jackson, copy a Florida tag: J John, M Michael, R Roger three, seven, nine. JMR three seven nine. Be out at Caroline and Lafayette."

"Ten-four, copy."

Aware of each other's every move, Joe and Pat left the patrol car for the clamor of the busy street. The sun was just sinking under the trees. Pat approached the passenger's side as Joe neared the driver.

"Driver, turn your engine off," Joe commanded the man through his open window.

"Can't you people leave me alone? I wasn't speeding; I didn't run a stop sign. Why the hell did you pull me over?" The man appeared to be in his mid-thirties. His speech was slurred, and Joe was able to distinguish the odor of an alcoholic beverage as he spoke. Joe glanced up at Pat, who remained unnoticed by the driver.

"Would you step out from the car, sir?" Joe was careful to note his movements while exiting, his difficulty getting out the door.

As the driver stepped onto the sidewalk, Steve, the midnight-shift officer who moved in to replace Kathleen on a permanent basis, drove up.

"Joe, they need you back at the station," Steve said, getting out of his patrol car. This guy drunk?" If Joe had to choose his new partner, he would have chosen Steve. He was bright and reliable—the two most important traits in a fellow officer.

"I haven't conducted field sobriety, but he reeks of beer. What's up at the station?" Joe was already uncomfortable.

"Don't really know. The chief's up there, though."

The chief didn't usually work past 4:30 if he could help it, but he was always in before six in the morning just to get a little work done before the daily rush. Something was up; Joe could feel it.

"Thanks, Steve. I'll give you my supplement for

this guy later," Joe said as he headed back to his car. Pat was right behind him.

There were a few important questions already on Joe's mind. Had they found Cyrus? Or his car? Of course, maybe they wanted him up there for something else entirely, but Joe didn't think so. Why else would Steve mention the chief being there? During the short drive, Pat and Joe said nothing. Pat was worried about him, about how he was handling Kathleen's death. They usually talked, but Pat was quiet, afraid that if he opened his mouth, Joe would crack into a million gloomy pieces.

Joe noticed the chief's car parked in its regular spot behind the station. At the back door he punched in the code that granted him access to the inner world of police work—a place he loved, a place Kathleen had loved.

"What's up, Wendy? What do you need?" He knew she needed nothing. Wendy pointed to the muster room. Joe, Pat, and Atlas walked in and found the chief staring out the room's only window.

"Hey, fellas. Sit down." The three men sat at the conference table; Atlas lay at Joe's feet.

"Got a bit of news. Seems they found Cyrus's truck. It had been rolled into one of the nearby lakes, Pike Lake, just west of town. Couple of kids found it when they were swimming. No obvious evidence. Just appears to have been pushed in the water over a week ago, as best they can tell. They dragged the lake, just to make sure Cyrus didn't go down with it, but they didn't find him. Looks as though whoever did it planned to sink the truck. Both windows open partway. They've towed it to the state police garage for further examination. Thought you'd want to hear it as soon as I knew."

Joe had never noticed before that the chief spoke

in cryptic sentences. Or was it just this occasion? "Thanks for letting me know. Anything on Cyrus?"

"No, nothing yet. They're doing all they can, Joe. I really believe that."

"Do her parents know yet?"

"Yeah, the sheriff said he already made that call. Said her mom took the news okay. It's not like we were expecting anything good there, you know."

"Right. Is that it?"

"All for now, Joe. Be careful out there." Those were always the chief's parting words.

Joe's and Pat's eyes met, though neither said a word. They marched out again, with the dog right behind them.

"That son of a bitch Cyrus."

"Yeah, that son of a bitch Cyrus." The words never left either man's lips, but they were having their first real conversation in a long while.

## CHAPTER VIII

Joe had no choice but to ask Pat for his help in moving Kathleen's furniture, and he wasn't eager to ask. He didn't want to return to her apartment, but had little choice. Mrs. Whibbs needed him to do this, and he wasn't about to let another member of that family down.

When Kathleen had moved from her old apartment to this, her last one, both Joe and Pat had been there to help. Joe jokingly accused her of buying furniture based not on appearance but on tonnage. He could hear her laughter as he and Pat struggled to shimmy the couch, tables, and big, unwieldy armchairs into the four small rooms of her new apartment. He never dreamed that one day he would be hauling the stuff out because she was never coming back in. And he dreaded making Pat a party to it.

"Pat, I hate to ask you, but Mrs. Whibbs wanted to give me some of Kathleen's furniture, and you know how heavy that stuff is. I can't do it alone. Do you have any time in the morning to help me move it? I'd need your truck, too." Joe could feel the sweat run under his vest.

"Sure, Joe, I'd be happy to help. How about ten?"

"That's fine. Meet me at my place, okay?"

Their plans had been set; Joe couldn't turn back now, so he drove. Drove up and down streets, looking for someone, anyone, to get Kathleen off his mind. But it started to rain, and the streets emptied of people and cars. Joe needed something to distract him from his thoughts, but the radio never cried out for him again.

After a fitful night's sleep, Joe got up and made a pot of strong coffee. He looked at his own furniture; the bachelor pad card table he used to eat on suddenly became an embarrassment to him. He wondered how Mrs. Whibbs knew he needed something more respectable, or was it something else? The dresser would fit easily in his bedroom. He used a steamer trunk to store most of his clothes. Although he made a good salary, he spent little on himself. Joe drove a five-year-old Jeep, lived frugally, and saved tremendously, preparing for a future he didn't yet know. He wondered how Jennifer would feel about his having Kathleen's furniture. He suspected she would accept it as she had accepted so much. He wanted to give her a call but just could not come up with words yet. She had left a few messages which he hadn't returned; he hoped she would hold on, wouldn't give up on him.

Pat arrived on time, as usual. Joe checked his pocket for the apartment key, and they set off. The drive was short, and they were both grateful—Pat because he was growing weary of the silence, and Joe because he wanted to escape the noises in his head. The parking space just outside Kathleen's door was vacant, and Pat backed his truck into her spot. Joe had never noticed the blinds that hung in the windows, probably because they were rarely closed all the way, as they were now. Joe told himself this would be the last time he would come here. He didn't want to be in Kathleen's space without her.

"Let's make this quick, Pat," he said as the key turned in the lock.

The lights were off, and with the blinds drawn, it seemed much later in the day. He flipped on the light switch, illuminating the main rooms of her apartment.

Joe half expected Mrs. Whibbs to have taken some small things at least, like a plant or picture frame, out of the apartment, but he was wrong. Everything was just as Kathleen had left it. Everything was like it should be, except that Kathleen wasn't here and never would be. Funny, Joe thought, how something as personal as a home didn't change when there was no longer a homeowner.

They walked to the kitchen table, tested its weight, and moved the four chairs against the wall, out of the way. The table was made of heavy knotty pine, worn by years of hard use. Kathleen had bought it at an auction, she had said, for a steal. Now Joe felt as though *he* were stealing it.

They placed it in the truck bed and pushed in the chairs around it so that it wouldn't shift, adding a blanket or carpet scrap here and there to cushion the load. There was enough room for the dresser, and they returned to get it, but as they approached her bedroom, Joe was struck by something. He paused at the door. "Pat, what if Mrs. Whibbs hasn't emptied it out? What if Kathleen's clothes are still in there?"

"Damn, I don't know. Surely she got them out already." Pat was not prepared to see Kathleen's more intimate possessions, and he was sure Joe wasn't, either.

They entered the bedroom with trepidation. The light radiated throughout the room. Joe had only passed this threshold a couple of times, and then only briefly. He was struck by the femininity here: the crisp white sheets folded back over a flowery comforter of white and pale yellow. Lace doilies protected the surface of the nightstands from the Tiffany-style lamps. There was a picture of her grandparents on top of the dresser, flanked by one of Joe and another of Kathleen, sitting alone atop a boulder in a canyon of red rock. They were fearful of opening the drawers, but out of impatience, Pat drew back a pull...empty. Joe pulled another. Nothing. They opened each drawer, and they found nothing. Joe removed the picture frames from the dresser and laid them facedown on the bed, but not before giving Kathleen a last look—another picture of her in a setting he did not recognize, a picture taken by a stranger.

They took out the drawers to make their load lighter, stacking each one next to the bed. With much grunting and straining, the two men hauled out another piece of Kathleen and tenderly brought it up to the bed of the truck. They moved it in close to the kitchen table and then returned for the empty drawers. Joe didn't know if he could fill them, didn't know if he could live with them. With a heavy cord they tied the load together and made certain it was secure. Joe turned out the bedroom light while Pat waited in the den, and they left her home together.

At Joe's place they had to reverse the process. There were two empty walls in his bedroom, and he decided to put the dresser next to the bed and not in front. He typically slept on his back, and didn't want to have to fall asleep in the shadow of her memory. Negotiating the heavy bureau through his doorway proved difficult, but finally they made the turn and settled it into its place. The kitchen table was easy. Joe just folded up his card table and stuck it in the hall closet. Although her table was bigger, it fit the space nicely, and he surprised himself at being comfortable with its presence. Pat didn't know what to say, so he begged off telling Joe he had some things to get done before work.

Alone, Joe poured himself a soda and sat down at his newly acquired table. He had sat in that same chair before, but never at the table alone. He couldn't function like this for much longer. His mind was not focused as it needed to be, especially on the job. And he was never going to help Kathleen if he was stuck in this fog. *Loss happens,* he said to himself. *Loss is life.* He'd never known it, not really, never faced it, but it had to be dealt with. One day he would be gone, too. It was a cycle, and perhaps, he thought, its point was to remind him of what could be left behind. He was leaving someone behind, and that, too, needed to change. He picked up the phone and called Jennifer. She answered, came over with Chinese food, and they broke bread and barriers over Kathleen's table.

## CHAPTER IX

Pat immediately sensed a turnaround in Joe. Even Atlas was more playful with him. Pat hoped it wasn't just an anomaly and that Joe had come to accept what had happened and would move on from there. Nothing positive could come of wallowing in pain. Because Pat was older and had experienced the loss of his mother, he knew that with time Joe's grief would diminish, although he would never forget it. Sorrow from loss never disappears, but it can soften and fade, he knew.

They talked. They discussed sports and weather and Jennifer. They joked about other officers who didn't quite make the muster. Joe and Pat seemed to be themselves for the most part, but the silences were more disturbing now, not quite so comfortable anymore.

Their shift was busy but uneventful. Nothing noteworthy happened, but they were on the go all night, answering calls for prowlers never found, drunk drivers never seen, and building alarms set off by the wind. The duo didn't have a chance to follow their favorite pursuit, drug pushers and users, but sometimes that was just how a shift might go.

Joe arrived at his apartment, no longer fearful of the memories that might greet him, but eager now to put some ideas down on paper about what he would do if he were in charge of Kathleen's murder investigation. He sat down at Kathleen's kitchen table and began to jot down notes:

*Family home:*
*Ellyson, site of grandmother's murder*

*Grandmother's murder:*
*Unsolved*

*Kathleen's murder:*
*Unsolved, on Cyrus Jackson's property*

*Cyrus:*
*Kathleen's cousin, missing*

Well, Joe thought, if I connect the dots, the path leads to Cyrus, the only common denominator. Could he have killed Kathleen's grandmother, too? And why? Kathleen must have learned something, perhaps confronted Cyrus with what she knew, and was killed because of it. But why had she done this alone? Maybe she overestimated her abilities. *Maybe I didn't teach her everything I should have,* he reflected. Or maybe she just had something to prove to herself. He didn't know. But he would find out.

Joe took a shower and decided to empty the contents of his footlocker into the drawers of Kathleen's dresser. Would he always refer to it as Kathleen's? No, he thought, not forever. Because of the limited space the footlocker provided, he had to stack his clothing and couldn't easily see what was at the bottom. Now he had a separate drawer for everything: underclothes, socks, T-shirts, shorts, jeans—everything had its proper place. He would keep the footlocker to store his seldom-worn sweaters. He wiped off the top of the dresser and took a picture of Jennifer from the living room and placed it on top. It looked lonely perched up there, so he added a silk plant his mother had given him. Better. With that, he lay down and fell asleep, unaware that the light was still on.

First thing in the morning, Joe called the sheriff's office. "Morning, Billy. Anything going on there I need to know about?" Joe was still in bed.

"No. Wish I could say different. Cyrus seems to have disappeared. Kathleen's duty weapon hasn't been found. It's frustrating. I know it's frustrating for you, too." Billy sounded sincere.

"Tell me, Billy, did Cyrus have a rap sheet?"

"Nothing official. He'd been stopped for drinking and public intoxication but never wound up in jail. He kept a pretty low profile, you know. Didn't go out much. Didn't do much. He didn't seem like a happy sort of fella, but that's about all I know about him." Like everyone else, Billy was sure Cyrus was guilty, too.

"What about family or friends? Surely he's got to have some somewhere?"

"Yeah, of course there's Kathleen's family — they're kin — but beyond that, we don't know. The sheriff talked to Mrs. Whibbs, but she couldn't help us. Bastard may be in Mexico by now. He didn't keep a checking account, no credit cards, either. Probably kept a stash of money in his shack. There's nothing to trace."

"I wonder, do you think the sheriff would let us go to Cyrus' house and poke around a little bit?" Joe deliberately included Billy in the mix, hoping that by asking him to join in, he'd push the sheriff a little harder to grant them access.

"Sure, I'll ask him. Couldn't hurt to have a couple more sets of eyes look around. Hang on." Billy covered the phone so Joe couldn't hear the conversation. "There's no active search warrant that would let us in. The sheriff says the police have checked every inch and found nothing. But he reminded me, what I do on my own time is my own business. I'm due some personal time. When are you coming over?" Billy sounded as eager as Joe.

"I just have to get dressed and drive over. I'm off today, so we could take our time, if that's okay with you."

"Just as long as nothing else is going on, and I doubt that would happen. See you in a couple, okay?"

"Great, Billy. I appreciate your help, man." Joe dressed in jeans and a T-shirt, each pulled from its separate drawer.

He put the top down on his Jeep for the drive this time. Joe noticed that whenever he drove with the wind in his face, the world appeared different. He could see not only from side to side but above as well. He could catch sight of the tops of the trees and buildings and water towers. His perspective changed, and he with it.

As he approached Ellyson on this trip, he noticed for the first time two churches that seemed to challenge each other. He caught a glimpse of a man high atop the spire of one, painting its front facade a brilliant white. The other church looked ignored, unloved, as suggested by its state of neglect – its chipped paint and unkempt lawn. It reminded him of Kathleen's grandmother's home—wholly overlooked.

Billy was outside the sheriff's office, eagerly awaiting Joe's appearance.

"Hey, Billy, ready to roll, or do I need to go inside the office first?" Joe glanced at the sky and decided it was safe to leave the top down.

"No, we're ready. I'll call in on my radio." Billy unlocked the passenger door for Joe and called in his departure from duty.

Along the way, Billy asked about Joe's

department. "How many officers do they have? How many sergeants? Do you have a K-9 unit?" Billy was awed to learn that Joe *was* the K-9 unit. His ongoing list of questions abruptly halted once they reached the turnoff. Set among tall pine trees, Cyrus's dilapidated shanty stood isolated from the street by its long dirt driveway. Around the house, even around the driveway, the land had been cleared. But for a few widely spaced trees, the settled part was blank space. Their mood turned somber as they neared the shack. The area was very still—no wind, no noise at all. Cyrus's dog had been given to the neighbor who lived on the other side of the swamp. He had offered to take care of him—knew the dog to be good on a duck hunt. Joe hadn't thought to ask how they would get in, but Billy answered his question by pulling out a key. Joe didn't know how he had come by it nor did he ask.

The inside was filthy. Dirt was scattered across the linoleum. The air conditioning unit hummed in the window. The shack consisted of four "rooms:" a bedroom, living room, kitchen, and bathroom. The main room had a single couch and an ancient recliner. The television, however, looked to be a recent purchase. An overturned apple crate served as the coffee table. It was bare but for a two-month-old issue of *Field and Stream*. In the kitchen Joe half expected to find dirty dishes piled in the sink, but found none. He opened cabinet doors and found cheap dishes of the kind you collect from the grocery store, neatly stacked.

"Look at this, Joe." Joe had forgotten that Billy was there. He walked to the refrigerator where Billy was standing. Inside were two six-packs of beer and a bottle of ketchup, nothing more. In the freezer compartment, there were about a dozen Hungry Man frozen dinners.

"Didn't entertain much, did he, Joe?" Billy chuckled softly.

"No, probably not the kind of person people want to spend time with." Joe moved on to the bedroom. The double bed was unmade. Joe was sure the sheets were meant to be white, but they were a dingy gray. Cyrus had a small two-drawer table in one corner. Joe went through the drawers but found little more than the standard utility bills and the title to Cyrus's truck. A small chest of drawers sat in the other corner. It contained a few T-shirts and some once-white socks and underwear. The closet held a few pairs of jeans, some old overalls, a pair of work boots, and three shirts. There were four empty hangers. Cyrus Johnson was not one for variety, it appeared. Two uniforms from his security job hung from a wooden dowel.

"Cyrus didn't have any friends from his job, Billy? Did you guys talk to them?" Joe noted the company name, Wilhoit.

"He worked alone. He had very little contact with their home office. They said he never missed a day, though, until now."

Joe was leery of going into the bathroom, afraid of the filth it surely held. It was tiny, just enough room for a toilet and shower. The plastic shower curtain was spotted with mildew, and dried mud lined the bottom of the tub. From its contents, the medicine cabinet told them only that Cyrus might have stomach problems, as it was full of half-used bottles of antacids. It occurred to Joe that there was nothing in the shack of a personal nature. Nothing hung on the walls—no family pictures, nothing that would evoke any kind of memory. Joe knew that Cyrus was an only child and therefore must have inherited all his mother's things, but nothing in the home suggested there was any family, past or present.

Joe had an idea. "Billy, I don't want to overlook anything. We need to check every square inch, even bang on the walls and make sure there's nothing hidden behind the paneling. Someone living like this has to have something to hide. We just have to find it." The two men methodically pounded on every inch of paneling. In the bedroom Billy found a sheet of paneling not flush with the others. The space between the two-by-fours contained several coffee cans, all of which were empty. Encouraged, Joe and Billy checked behind doors and under furniture, poking around in every nook until they were certain nothing was there.

The shack had two doors; one led to the swamp, and the other, the way they had come in, led to the driveway. There was no shed or garage, no other structure of any sort, so they walked in a loose grid pattern, covering the entire area back to the swamp and then up to the road. Most of the ground was hard and flat, void of anything green or colorful, and it gave them nothing, nothing that would help lead them to Cyrus.

Just as they were getting ready to leave, Joe turned back toward the swamp. "Has anyone checked back there, Billy? Has anyone looked around?"

"As far as I know, just the area around where I found Kathleen. Maybe the state police did, but I don't know."

"Well, we've come this far; why don't we hunt around there for a bit? We've got nothing to lose, right?" Joe hoped he still had an ally.

"No problem, but I've got to get something to eat and drink first. I'm dying. It's after lunch time, you know." Billy seemed to be losing some of his humor.

"Sure, Billy, my treat. There is a restaurant

around here, right?" Joe had never noticed one during his drives.

"Yeah, Emily's Diner has good home cooking. You've got to try her chicken-fried steak." Billy was clearly taxed by their work this morning; his hair was matted by the sweat.

"Sounds good. Let's go." Not that Joe liked that kind of food, but he now noticed that he was feeling a bit hungry himself.

The aroma just outside the front door to Emily's told Joe that he would be treated to deep-southern food. He glanced around and saw tables laden with corn bread, fried okra, biscuits, and collard greens—foods he had never really developed a taste for. But Joe didn't mind. Someone had invited him into this world, and who was he to judge it?

They sat down on black vinyl bar stools at the counter. They both ordered chicken fried steak, Billy's with a side of okra, and Joe's with fresh green beans. Joe ate ravenously and didn't notice Billy's stare.

"Good food, huh? They have anything like this back in Florida?" Billy ordered peach cobbler as the waitress cleared their plates.

"Not around where I live." Joe wasn't sure how true that was, but he had never paid much attention to the country-cooking kinds of places. "Boy, that was good. I think I'll have some cobbler, too, with vanilla ice cream on top." Billy was sure he had met a kindred spirit.

Over coffee, Joe tried to pick Billy's brain. "Okay, so if Cyrus didn't leave in Kathleen's car or his own car, how did he get out of town? There's no train, right?"

"Used to be, but they don't run through here anymore. He could have walked, I suppose, but after all the stories in the press, if someone had seen him on the road, we would have been told. I guess he could have hitchhiked, but I don't think he would have done that if he had been on the run. No, if I were trying to get out of town without my own wheels, I would borrow some, maybe even steal some. But we haven't received any reports of cars missing." Billy looked perplexed.

"Maybe he never left town."

Billy's face grew serious at Joe's suggestion. "No one in Ellyson would hide him. They know better. I don't think Cyrus even had a friend he could call on. Nah, I don't think he's here. Too many people looking out for him." Joe had no choice but to agree.

"He wouldn't have killed himself, you think?" Joe knew he was reaching, but none of the scenarios they had discussed seemed likely.

"If he'd done that, we would know. I don't think he would have dragged himself out to some forest and left his body for the animals, know what I mean? He would have made it plain." They rose from the counter, Joe paid for their lunch, and together they headed back toward Cyrus's property.

Along the way, Billy radioed the sheriff to find out if he had heard any news. "No, Billy, nothing. But that will change. If not today, tomorrow or the next day. He's not going to get away with this." He gave the weary searchers his blessings and told them to call in at the end of Billy's regular shift, now just three hours away — the last hours of daylight.

A curtain of tangled shadows loomed on the untamed side of Cyrus' property. As they followed the ruts of the driveway, Joe concentrated on this definitive door to the swamp, the same swamp that had witnessed Kathleen's murder. Billy grabbed his flashlight and took an extra one out of a fishing tackle box in his trunk.

"Snakes and gators?" asked Joe as they started into the steaming vegetation.

"Snakes, but no gators. Just keep your eyes open in there, okay?"

*Like I wouldn't,* Joe thought. For over an hour they continued their serpentine search, their path jumping over broken limbs and ducking thick vines. Other times, just to make room to walk, Billy, who led, carved out space with his flashlight, banging his way through the briars. Joe scanned around and above with Billy's Maglite; the dense trees appeared to tower overhead, a canopy of branches. He wondered if this invisible man was there, lurking among the branches, laughing to himself about how clumsily they hunted below.

Finally, they gave up, defeated by exhaustion and diminishing light. They had seen nothing but nature, no suggestion a human being, other than Kathleen, had been near. And with the crime scene tape gone, it was hard to tell even where *she* had been. But during all the turning and backtracking, they lost all sense of direction. Neither sound nor marker was distinguishable. No trails were evident. Each tree resembled the other. Every broken limb looked like the next. The terrain showed no foot prints; every step had been absorbed by the muck. But Billy caught sight of the last beams of the sun and from that, they turned toward the west, the direction of the shack. As they made their way back through the web of vegetation, neither one talked, either from fatigue or discouragement. Joe began to strip off all the intensity that maintained him during the search–anxiety, expectation, heightened senses–and he loosened his concentration. He then began to realize how dry his mouth was, how much his neck ached, how coated with sweat he was. Joe numbly followed Billy, who seemed to numbly follow the fading daylight. Once Joe breached the swamp, left the shadows and entered the red-lit dusk, he was struck with the sensation that he had regained his sense of self, his gut instinct for understanding a criminal—and this time it would be the murderer of his friend. He didn't know if visiting the scene of Kathleen's last breath brought about the change, but he felt whole again, like himself. Somehow, it was as if Kathleen had something to do with it. But he opted not to share his revelation with Billy.

## CHAPTER X

After thanking Billy for his time and trouble, Joe jumped in his Jeep to head home. Cyrus was still in or near Ellyson. He was certain of it for two reasons: Cyrus had nowhere to go, but he had to go somewhere. Joe felt like Cyrus could probably survive in the elements for an extended period of time. He had noticed one broken fishing pole inside the house. People around here hunted and fished, and Cyrus probably did, too, yet none of that gear was at his home. No camping equipment, nothing like it. There were no non-perishables in the kitchen. Surely the man would have had at least a can of baked beans in the house, but they found nothing when they searched. There were more clues to be found in what Cyrus's house lacked rather than in what it held.

Why didn't he want to tell Billy his thoughts? Joe didn't fully trust him, he decided. Not that Billy gave him any reason, but Joe was out of his element, and he didn't know all the players.

Joe thought about all the undeveloped land, and there was a lot of it, around Ellyson—Cyrus was holed up out there somewhere, in just the right spot, a virtual speck in a sea of green-topped trees. But he would occasionally have to go to a store for something, and it wouldn't be in Ellyson. Joe needed a map of the area to find the nearest towns and work from there. He liked having the top down; he could see so much more.

He returned to Jackson and, not trusting the weather there, snapped the panels back together once he reached the parking lot at the apartment complex. Two messages blinked on his answering machine: one from Pat, just checking to see how he was, and the other from Jennifer, wondering the same. He would call Jennifer back tonight and Pat back tomorrow.

He filled Jennifer in on the search, but not on his theory. Joe didn't know what his next move should be, and until then he didn't want to worry her or disappoint her if he was wrong. After he hung up, he logged on to his computer to look for a map of the area surrounding Ellyson. Within a few minutes, he had the names of two towns that were possibilities: Newton, seven miles to the west, and Calvert, nine miles northeast. The other towns were more than fifteen miles away, and if Joe was right, Cyrus wouldn't know those areas as well. With another day off tomorrow, he decided to head up to both places and do a little snooping. He had a picture of Cyrus, the one from Cyrus's security badge, and it would give him something to show around, something to start with.

The next morning, the weather changed. Ominous-looking thunderstorms gathered to the west. A front was moving in, and it appeared to be a violent but fast-moving one. Joe checked in with Pat, telling him only briefly about yesterday and his plans for the afternoon. He didn't tell him, however, that he would be looking outside Ellyson. *Isn't that just what Kathleen did?* he asked himself as he hung up the phone. *Not tell anyone what she was doing?* He knew it was true, but he also knew he wasn't ready to change his plan.

The drive took quite a bit longer in the pouring rain and frequent lightning. The rain came down in sheets, at times momentarily robbing Joe of his vision ahead. He plowed on, witnessing the debris of two recent car crashes. How he hated to work on days like these, spending his shift driving from accident to accident. He was happy to have the day off. He headed first for Newton, a town he'd never known existed.

The word "town" was a bit of an exaggeration. Newton was even smaller than Ellyson, if that were possible. A small savings and loan, a drugstore, and a mom-and-pop market were the only commercial businesses he saw in what must once have been downtown. He skipped the S and L and headed for the pharmacy. He seemed to be the only customer, and then again, not that.

"Morning. I'm hoping you can help me, sir. I'm looking for a man, and I've got a picture of him. It's not great, but maybe you recognize him." The man behind the counter didn't seem very approachable.

"You the law?" he asked as he glanced at Joe's folded photo.

"Nah, I represent his mother's estate, and he has some land coming to him. Thought he lived in these parts, somewhere here in South Alabama, but I haven't had much luck." Cops were allowed to lie.

"Doesn't strike me as someone I've ever seen. Sorry I couldn't help you. Do you have a card?"

Joe hadn't banked on getting that question, but he thought quickly. "You know, when I put this man's papers in my briefcase, I completely forgot to put in my business cards. I'll leave you my number, though." Joe wasn't sure he bought it, but with a steady hand he jotted down his cell phone number.

"From Florida, huh?" He seemed more amenable now.

"Yes, sir. Are there any good restaurants nearby? I just love southern cooking."

"Just one. The Carmichael Inn. Fried catfish is

their specialty. Take a right here and you'll see it just past the gas station. Can't miss it." Joe thought he detected some of the chill melting away.

"Thanks. Sounds just like what I'm looking for."

Joe chuckled as he made the quick drive to the restaurant. The gas station, an independent holdout, sold gasoline and diesel, of course, but also sandwiches, tackle, "minners," camping gear, and boiled peanuts, according to the various hand-painted signs hanging from its windows and doors. A one-stop shop for sure, Joe thought.

It was just after eleven, and the restaurant had few customers. Joe walked to the counter, toward an attractive waitress. "Good morning. I understand you have some wonderful catfish dinners here. I haven't had one of those in a while." He wouldn't give her a chance to comment. "By the way, have you seen anyone who resembles this?" Joe produced the picture from his pocket. "His mother left him some land, and I'm trying to find him and let him know."

Her eyes widened. "He doesn't look familiar, and I don't forget a face — that is, I never forget a *handsome* one — but still, I don't think he's been here." Joe thought he detected some form of flirtation.

"Well, if you don't mind, if he should come in here, will you call me at this number? It's my personal cell phone." Joe barely emphasized the word "personal." He thought in the next second, however, that he might have made a tactical mistake — she might call just to chat. "I'd also like an order of your catfish."

Joe dined in silence, although he fielded many glances from the woman whose name tag read "Christina." After leaving a generous tip, he drove back to the gas station to try his luck with Cyrus's picture.

The atmosphere there was decidedly different. Two men seemed to run the place, and they appeared to be identical twins. Standing there behind the bait tank, they looked formidable.

"Afternoon, gentlemen. I need to fill up my car. What credit cards do you take?" It was the wrong thing to say.

"We don't take plastic. If you don't have real money, you ain't buying gas from here," scowled the brother wearing the camouflage ball cap.

Joe tried to redeem himself. "I've got cash, too— no problem." Joe thought they looked disappointed, and by their tone, he wasn't eager to pull out Cyrus's picture. But he had to. "Wonder if you fellas have ever seen this character. His mother left him some land, and he used to live around these parts, but I'm having trouble finding him."

They both held the picture. Joe didn't see any signs of recognition on their faces. "No," said the hat-wearing brother, "he ain't never been here."

"Well, thanks anyway. I'll put twenty dollars in my car and be on my way." Joe produced the bill and handed it to the other brother, who promptly walked to the register and dropped it in. "Have a nice afternoon," Joe shot back as he left the building. The one with the cap walked outside just before Joe pulled away and watched him drive off. The clouds were just clearing overhead.

After those two encounters, Joe traversed Newton's few streets, looking for any kind of establishment Cyrus might want to visit. There was nothing else. He began to grow fearful that his hunch was wrong, and he was just wasting his time.

It took nearly an hour to reach Calvert, not that the distance was great, but there were a couple out-of-the-way gas stations along the way, and Joe wanted to check them out. Nothing. No one had seen Cyrus; at least, that's what they told him. Calvert was a bit bigger than Ellyson, bigger even than Joe had expected. Once he arrived in the center of town, he saw at least three restaurants and a handful of stores that Cyrus might want to call on. He decided to do his snooping on foot, and he parked his car outside an auto parts store. He had no luck there or at the restaurant next door. No one at the drugstore could help, either. Everywhere it was the same story. No one had seen Cyrus, and Joe believed them. He never noted any deception from anyone, and Joe prided himself on his ability to read faces.

Disgusted and discouraged, he had little choice other than to return home, regroup, and rethink. Because he had come over on a different highway, he checked out a couple of places along the way back, but no one offered him any hope. Joe hadn't given up, though. Joe never did.

# CHAPTER XI

Joe slept more that night than he had in weeks. He didn't wake up until after ten and didn't roll out of bed for another half hour. The past couple of days had taxed his mind and body, and he realized he needed the rest. After eating what he considered a healthy breakfast after all the recent fried food, he threw on some old shorts and a T-shirt and headed outside with soap and a bucket to wash his car. The wet roads had kicked up mud on the Jeep's undercarriage, and he liked to keep his car clean. If he waited much longer, the muck would dry and he would have to scrub it off, which was tough on paint. The spray from the nozzle slowly dissolved the earth and washed her down the parking lot toward a storm sewer. Joe contemplated how, with just the addition of water, he could change the nature of a semisolid to something he could wash away with a focused stream, sending it right down into the earth. It was what he wanted to do with Cyrus.

He called Jennifer at work, showered, and met her for lunch at La Hacienda, one of their favorite restaurants. Jennifer believed Joe was getting back to his old self, and Joe saw himself as someone completely changed, someone who was not moving on but moving through and around and under—a guy transforming into a man.

While he and Jennifer were at lunch, Pat called his cell phone and told him he couldn't work with him tonight because something had come up at home. Joe translated: his wife wanted him home. Joe understood. Pat worked full-time at another job and often donned a police uniform in the evenings, so that left little time to spend with family.

Wendy was working as the dispatcher, and her presence almost always put Joe in a good mood. "Miss me, Wendy?" They both knew his flirtations were harmless.

"You? No," she giggled. "Atlas, yes." Atlas set his muzzle on her palm so she would pet him.

"Been that busy?" Joe asked as he looked over the pass-down.

"Not really. Same old stuff, same old people. I don't have to tell you that."

"Nope, some things never change."

Wendy started to ask him if he'd heard any more about Kathleen's case, but she didn't want to spoil his mood. "Pat working tonight?"

"No. Family night. Atlas, car. Call if you need anything, Wendy." Joe was eager to get to work. He had fewer arrests than anyone this month, and even though everyone knew why, Joe usually had the most, and he didn't like the feeling that he wasn't doing his job. He passed Steve in the hallway.

"Ready to roll, Steve?"

"I'll catch up. See you on the streets." Steve smiled as he walked on to speak to Wendy. He sensed a change in Joe as well.

During the first part of his shift, Joe conducted walk-and-talks, dropping in on businesses to see if they were having any problems that the police should be aware of. Other than the occasional vagrant and a couple of renegade skateboarders, no one had too much to complain about. Joe visited several strip malls and listened to some complaints about trash dumped outside the merchants' doors, but there was little else. As five o'clock neared, Joe decided to shift his attention.

After filling up his patrol car, he headed for his favorite area, what he called "drugville." With him not keeping up patrols lately, more people seemed to be milling around outside. "That's okay, as long as they remain upstanding, law-abiding individuals," Joe said out loud, as though Pat were there or Atlas understood sarcasm.

No sooner had the words left his mouth than he heard what sounded like gunfire aimed at his car. Joe jumped, startled at the sound he hadn't heard since Kathleen's funeral. In reality, it was a couple of firecrackers, though the knowledge did not stop the adrenaline that shot through his body, giving him that familiar feeling he always experienced after a high-speed chase or a lengthy fight with a bad guy. But Joe didn't see much distinction after he slammed on his breaks and ducked under the steering wheel. Peering out, he saw that everyone around the apartment complex scooted indoors, and Joe, along with a barking Atlas, was left alone in the parking lot. *Son of a bitch*, he said out loud as though Pat were there or Atlas understood curse words.

He drove his car around the corner and started checking license plates on his mobile data terminal, or as the officers call it, the laptop. The introduction of the laptop in the police car is both a blessing and a bane to officers. They are sometimes problematic because now the police officer has one more piece of equipment to operate concurrently with all the others, such as lights, sirens, radios, all of which must be managed while driving the car at high speeds. But on the other hand, the laptop is an information gold mine.

Joe randomly entered plates, checking to make sure the plate matched the vehicle. The second one he ran didn't match. The plate came back to a Chevrolet Corsica, but it was on a Toyota Celica. That would give him reason enough to stop the vehicle, but at the moment it was parked and unoccupied. Joe made a mental note to look out for the car during his patrol. He quickly found an expired tag, and this car, too, was parked and empty. But he would keep an eye out. As he drove slowly by, he noticed in his rear view mirror two men approaching the first car. They slowed their gait once they noticed Joe, quickly turned around, and ducked back into an apartment. "Next time," Joe thought to himself.

Over the radio, Steve called out a traffic stop of a vehicle on Dunlop Street. The car was occupied by four subjects. Those weren't the best odds, so Joe decided to drive by just to make sure they didn't give Steve any trouble. As he turned his patrol car around, Steve frantically called out over the radio for backup. "They're running. East on Mallory." *Give me more,* Joe thought to himself, all the while understanding how difficult it was to call out a location while running at top speed with thirty pounds of gear. "South on Prescott." Joe was near that intersection, and he caught a glimpse of two males running in his direction. They shot back west on Detroit when they noticed Joe's car. Atlas was inconsolable. He wanted to run his own chase, but his aluminum cage held him back. Apartments lined both sides of the street, and once Joe made the turn, the two men had disappeared. Steve wasn't there, either, and he hadn't called out on the radio.

"Unit nine to unit fourteen. What's your twenty?" The silence was followed by radio static and then silence again. "Unit fourteen, what's your twenty?" Joe's voice was louder this time, growing more concerned about his fellow officer, not wanting to lose someone else.

"Prescott." The voice was weak.

"Ten-four, unit fourteen. Ten fifty-one. Hang on." Joe blew in reverse down Detroit and spun around onto Prescott. He flipped on his light bar as well as the spotlight and illuminated both sides of the street, looking for Steve. Still he saw nothing. "Unit fourteen, what's your twenty?" Joe was exasperated by now. Didn't Steve know his location? Was he hurt? Or worse?

Just then he noticed a reflection near a chain-link fence next to the road. Looking more closely, he confirmed that it was a body, a body in uniform. He threw the car in park and ran up to him. Steve was laying facedown. In disbelief at the turn of events, Joe tentatively reached down to check his carotid artery for a pulse. The heartbeat was strong. *Thank God,* thought Joe. He rolled his partner over and was grateful to see him stirring.

"What the hell happened?" Joe helped lift him to a sitting position. Before Steve could answer, Wendy radioed.

"Unit nine, everything ten-four?" Joe knew she was worried.

"Ten-four. Unit fourteen is ten-four. Roll EMS, though." He wanted the medics on site. Joe noticed swelling just above Steve's right eye. It was oblong, not the kind of mark a fist would make. "So what happened? You feel okay?"

"Yeah, my head hurts a little, here," he said as he gently touched the growing bulge on his face. "I'll be okay. I think the bastard hit me with a bat or something. I have just a vague memory of it. I was chasing the driver because I lost the other three, and he ran around this corner. I swung wide to clear it, but he was waiting for me." Steve tried to stand but lost strength before he got up off the ground.

Joe could hear the ambulance's siren in the near distance. He got a description of the driver and sent out the BOLO for a white male, early twenties, with a goatee, wearing a white T-shirt and black jeans. He sent out one for the two who had run from him as well, but nothing on the fourth. Steve had no description of him. Once the paramedics arrived, Joe returned to Dunlop Street to check out the foursome's abandoned vehicle and secure Steve's patrol car. If the scene didn't get contaminated, he would return to Steve's location and use Atlas to track them. But with only him on duty now, it was unlikely they could use that resource. There was no registration in the car, but he did find a crack pipe and a small paper bag full of marijuana.

Joe radioed Wendy with the VIN number of the car and learned that it was registered to a Perry Hutchinson of Holly, Florida. A wants-and-warrants check revealed that he was wanted in Holly for burglary, theft, and grand larceny. Joe called dispatch again, this time to request a tow truck for Perry's car and to request that either Tony or Adam, the midnight-shift guys, get in early to help out with the last two hours of the shift. Tony volunteered and met Joe at the police station to go and pick up Steve's car.

The ambulance took Steve to the hospital for X-rays, but Joe had no word yet on his condition. Wendy notified the chief at home of the incident, and he, too, was awaiting word on Steve's status. Wendy told Joe that the only words that left the chief's mouth were "Damn it." Nothing else. The fear of losing another officer was apparent not only in the chief's demeanor, but also in everyone who worked there. Kathleen had been murdered not long ago, and they were all a little jumpy. No one was surprised to hear the chief decided to check on Steve himself, and both he and Joe got there at the same time.

"What the hell happened, Joe? You were on your way to back him up, right?" The chief was clearly aggravated, and Joe wasn't sure if he was testing Joe's police skills or just inquiring about what he heard over the scanner.

"Yes, sir. They bailed before I got there. Steve was calling out his location on foot, and I found two of them. When I couldn't raise him on the radio, I started backtracking." Both Joe and the chief knew that Joe had done nothing wrong. Sometimes things just go bad, and there's not always someone to blame, other than the bad guy. But still, Joe felt his own guilt. He hadn't been there for another officer—another officer who got hurt. He felt responsible, and he was beginning to feel jinxed.

The ambulance bay doors welcomed them. Steve was just returning in a wheelchair from X-ray as they walked into the emergency department. Joe was taken aback by the size of the welt on Steve's head, and the chief was even more shocked, not having seen the earlier version of the swelling. Still, Steve was talking and joking about the incident. "Did you bring me a steak? Figured I'd tenderize it on my face for a while and then cook it up for dinner." Both Joe and the chief were relieved when a nurse placed an ice pack over the injury. Dr. Sall entered through the closed curtains.

"Well, you are one lucky son of a gun. No bleeding on the brain. No fractured skull. The only thing we have to worry about is that you probably did suffer a concussion. Do you have anyone at home? You can't be alone tonight. You need someone to check on you every couple of hours."

Steve wasn't married, but he had a girlfriend, Megan. He had begged Joe not to call her earlier, and Joe had grudgingly acquiesced.

"No, but I could call my girlfriend to come over if it's important. I wouldn't want the chief to babysit me." They all chuckled. It was agreed that Steve would call Megan and forewarn her of his appearance. The doctor prescribed blood-thinning medication as well as some pain pills, which Joe volunteered to pick up at the hospital pharmacy. He arrived just in time to catch Megan's tears. The tug of guilt pulled at him again. He quietly dropped off the medicine and left, but the chief noticed. He also understood.

## CHAPTER XII

Joe was shaky. He thought for a while that he had handled it, but realized he couldn't rid himself of the shadow of Kathleen and her death, not yet anyway, and perhaps he never would. It followed him like the trail of icing on a still-warm cake. He knew intellectually that he had done nothing wrong in either situation, Kathleen's or Steve's, yet they had both been hurt on his watch. No, he corrected himself, Kathleen had gone her own way, done her own thing. And she paid the price for that independence. That was something beyond his control. He was reminded of one particular night, soon after she had gained her freedom from him as her field training officer—a story that Kathleen was a little too fond of telling.

It was the third of July, hot and sultry as Julys usually are in the South. Kathleen had driven to one of her favorite areas for dope busting. Folks were out in the street that night, doing a little pre-celebration celebrating. Just as she passed the crowd, someone threw a bottle rocket right behind her car—not unlike what had recently happened to Joe in the firecracker incident. Kathleen slammed on her brakes and backed up in the street, right in front of the crowd. They were all laughing uproariously at their prank, but Kathleen saw little humor.

"You know bottle rockets are illegal here. Don't let me see another one, y'all understand?" They just laughed, which made Kathleen all the more angry. She decided to keep an eye on them and drove about half a block down the road, turned around, and parked on the side of the street next to an abandoned house. She got out of her vehicle and sat on the hood of her car just to watch them. Kathleen didn't tell dispatch what she was up to, and in the meantime, Joe and Pat were on their own patrol. Her anger subsided, and Kathleen enjoyed watching the kids play with their sparklers and run from little firecrackers. But not long afterward, someone launched another bottle rocket, which went straight up into the air. It followed the same path back but, unfortunately, practically exploded in the face of a man standing in the street. He screamed, which aroused the entire growing crowd. Kathleen jumped in her car and drove to his vicinity to check on him. He laughed and said he was just fine, and by the slur in his voice, Kathleen was sure he felt no pain. But the event proved her point.

"You all saw what happened. The next one to set off a bottle rocket is going to wind up in the back of my car. I don't want someone to get hurt." But the crowd was not accommodating. By this time, over fifty people were out in the street, mostly surrounding her car. A known dealer, Frankie, approached Kathleen who had returned to her perch on the hood of her car.

"What you gonna do if we all pull out our guns and shoot your ass?" he hissed at her. Kathleen said she could almost taste his breath.

"Take you and a few of your close personal friends with me." She could feel the sweat pouring down her chest beneath the Kevlar and the cotton T-shirt. Only then did she decide she might need help.

"Unit eighteen to unit nine. What's your twenty?"

"Lincoln and Baxter."

"When you're not busy, you mind coming down my way?"

"Ten-four. ETA five."

Kathleen thought to herself that a lot could happen in five minutes, and none of it good. She was in a high state of alert, but she knew that if she jumped in her car and sped away as every bone in her body begged her to, they would know she was weak and scared. Being new on the job, there was no way she would let them have that impression. So she waited, hand relaxed over her gun, poised and ready to unsnap her holster in an instant if the situation arose. Her eyes were moving in all directions, looking at hands, looking for anything that could threaten her. The crowd had become so loud, Kathleen could no longer hear any traffic over her shoulder mike. But out of the corner of her eye, she noticed the crowd in the street begin to part, and she swore to herself it must be Moses. It was, in the forms of Joe and Pat and Atlas, and she began to breathe again.

Over the loudspeaker she could make out Joe saying, "Return to your homes. If you do not return to your homes and get off the streets, you will be placed under arrest." He repeated the warning several times but was only successful in getting them off the street. Joe decided more help was needed, so he asked Wendy to call the county to assist. Kathleen had single-handedly started a riot. Joe didn't know if he should pat her on the back or knock her to the ground, so he did neither.

"What the hell have you been doing? Didn't I teach you anything? You can't handle a crowd like this alone." Joe was in her face.

"I know. That's why I called you." He could sense a scam coming. "I was fine. I just thought I should have backup, you know, just in case." Joe knew she was lying.

The sweat along her brow streamed down the side of her face. She was pale.

The county showed up moments later with seven patrol cars. They lined the street with lights flashing, and after about five minutes the crowd dispersed but not before someone hurled a few beer bottles into the road. Kathleen earned a reputation that night with law enforcement and with those she would enforce: "crazy woman" and "crazy bitch," respectively.

*Yes, crazy* stupid *woman,* Joe thought to himself. And what about Steve? Shouldn't he have waited until Joe got there to go after those guys? No, he admitted. No cop would wait. Waiting cost lives and arrests and opportunities. Steve should have checked around that corner before he followed. But all cops did it from time to time. Steve just got caught. "Not my fault," he said, this time out loud, but he still wasn't convinced.

The midnight shift picked up the slack of the evening shift, and Joe got home right at ten. He called Steve's apartment to check on him. Megan told him he was doing fine and that she would call if she needed help. Joe didn't detect anger or disappointment in her voice, and he was grateful. He showered quickly and realized he had never had dinner. He considered calling Jennifer and going out for pizza, but decided it was too late. He made himself a peanut butter and jelly sandwich and ate it at Kathleen's table. "Kathleen's table," he said to himself again. He hoped he would stop thinking of it that way some day. Not to obliterate the memory of her, but to cast the memory of her from his house. No, not even that, really. It was just that he longed for a time when everything wasn't judged in relation to Kathleen. But she permeated him: his home, his thoughts, his work, and now his life. He couldn't be there for Kathleen that night, but he could be there for her tomorrow. Finding Cyrus would bring him peace. He fell asleep planning his course, with Atlas at his side.

## CHAPTER XIII

No one had to know that Atlas was a police dog. Joe slipped the badge from his collar and stuck it in his back pocket. Top down, windows halfway up, Joe and Atlas headed for Ellyson, but not before checking in on Steve.

"No, bud, pain pills put me right out, although Megan kept waking me up to check on me. I have a little headache, but brother, do I ever look like hell. Half of my forehead is blue, and not a pretty shade, either." Joe was grateful his sense of humor wasn't knocked out of him. "I'll be there today. Hope I don't scare you to death." Not a good word choice there, Joe thought to himself.

Atlas loved riding in the Jeep. No longer confined to the back of the car, he luxuriated in the shotgun position. Because of his size, he could not lie down comfortably, but he would have chosen to sit up in any case, not wanting to miss any of the sights.

Joe bypassed the sheriff's office and headed straight to Cyrus's house. He vaguely remembered some articles of clothing outside the shack, which he and Billy never checked for any telltale clues—not that Joe was optimistic about finding something meaningful, but he didn't want to leave anything unchecked. He was acutely aware that if his search proved productive, it wouldn't matter, not to the DA, anyway. There was no search warrant to cover his visit. But he didn't care. He was looking for himself and not the law. He remembered at least one pair of work boots just outside the back door.

Once Joe arrived at the top of the driveway, his heart began to beat faster, something Atlas must have sensed because his excitement rose as well. As they walked around the building, Joe spotted the boots and a forgotten towel next to them.

Atlas loved to play tug-of-war. It didn't matter if the object were a stuffed animal, a sock, or a chew toy, he loved getting down on his haunches and pulling with all his strength. He was strong, too. Joe remembered when he once had Kathleen wear the sleeve to help train Atlas to take down a suspect. She was happy to help out until she turned around wearing that oversized burlap-covered, reinforced sleeve that seemed to swallow her body. She didn't like the look on Atlas's face. He ceased to recognize her as a friend. Joe told her to run, which she gladly did, but as she heard Atlas growling and closing the distance behind her, Kathleen began to scream. In one quick leap, Atlas pulled her by that arm to the ground and tugged at the bite sleeve, trying to wrestle it from her.

"Damn, Joe, that scared me to death!" Kathleen yelled at him as he called Atlas off her. "Don't ask me to be your dummy again, got it?" Joe couldn't help but chuckle as she flicked off the dewy grass from her uniform. "That was a terrifying feeling, seeing him like that. It felt like Cujo was after me," she had said, only half laughing. Another time Joe persuaded Kathleen to hide in one of several wooden boxes placed sporadically throughout a field. The test would show whether Atlas could figure out which container she hid in.

"This sure beats having him chase me down," she said, still not fully recovered from the memory of the chase. But when Joe opened up the box for her to get in, Kathleen was welcomed with a cluster of spider webs.

"No way am I getting in there with all those spiders, Joe. Forget it." Joe couldn't believe a woman who would stand up to a crowd of mean drunks would cower at the prospect of something so small.

Joe laughed, took out his flashlight, and cleared the space for her. Kathleen reluctantly got in, and Joe slammed the door. She didn't utter a sound until after Atlas alerted, and Joe let her out.

"I am through doing this kind of work, mister. Not in the job description. Never again, got it?"

Joe half believed her.

Daydream over, Joe let Atlas off lead. "Here, boy, look at this." Joe was pointing toward the towel. "What's that, boy? What's that?" Atlas couldn't resist the temptation to pick up the towel and wave it at Joe, begging him to play with him, but not before Joe looked for a label or anything that could tell him something. There was nothing. Once Atlas got hold of it, Joe pulled on it for a minute of play, then turned his attention to the boots.

"What's that, boy? What's that?" Joe looked inside the tan steel-toed boots. They were a Chippewa brand, but he couldn't determine the size, although they looked a little larger than his own size 10 boots. Beyond some dried dirt stuck in the soles, there was nothing else to tell from them. Joe walked the perimeter of the house, looking for something else that could help, but found nothing more. "Come on, boy. Let's go." Atlas jumped back into the Jeep, the towel still in his jaws. Joe didn't care. "Good boy. Good boy." Joe rubbed his ears as they drove back up the driveway toward a more populated area.

Not five minutes from Cyrus's home, Joe's cell phone rang. He didn't recognize the number, but it had an Alabama area code.

"Hello?"

The voice was young and female and very southern. "Yes, sir. You left your card with me just in case I saw that man in your picture. Well, I think I did, so I'm calling to let you know."

"Right. You work at the diner, don't you?"

"Yes. You remember me?"

"Sure, I do. Christina, right? Tell me, how long ago did you see him?"

"Maybe thirty minutes. I couldn't find your number right away. Anyway, he looked a little like he hadn't had a bath in a while, and he was pretty hungry, too. He had a beard and a mustache working, which threw me off for a bit, but I recognized his eyes."

"How did he leave? Did he have a car or did he walk?" Joe was on his way, about twenty minutes from the diner.

"He walked away from town. I couldn't see where he went once he walked by the window, because I had customers."

"What was he wearing?" Joe was nearly salivating.

"Jeans and a black T-shirt."

"Was he alone at the diner?"

"Yes."

"Are you sure it was him?"

She hesitated. "I think so. I'm pretty sure."

"Well, Christina, you've been a great help to me. I'm close to your neighborhood, so I'll drive around and see if I can find him. I'll make him a wealthy man." Joe didn't like lying to her, but he had to. "If I have time, I'll swing by and get a piece of pie from you."

"Oh, okay. I'll be here until four. The blueberry's

freshest."

Joe strained his eyes, looking for Cyrus. He traversed the community for over an hour but saw no sign of him. There were trails everywhere that led to dense woods, and Joe couldn't travel them all. But he had an idea now about where his quarry could be – there was too much land to cover, so he decided to come back again later to look. But he felt his gut was right – Cyrus hadn't left the area. The pie would have to wait.

Joe and Atlas returned home tired and disappointed, but Joe felt better doing something proactive, even if it was a long shot into nothingness. Back at home, he let Atlas have a much needed rest and water to get ready for a night's work on the street. Joe was less than energetic, but Pat left a message that he would work with him tonight. Joe needed the extra set of eyes and ears. His were spent.

He resumed his walk-and-talks at the businesses he didn't visit the day before. Their complaints were much the same, although the owner of Tom's Electronics pointed out that someone had attempted to jimmy open his back door. Joe took a look and agreed that someone had tampered with it, and he promised to do some drive-bys during the shift.

Pat joined him at six after he had an early dinner with his family. Pat made no excuses about spending time with them. "When you have a family one day, you'll understand," Pat would tell him, often. "You're not going to want to leave the comfort of your home." Joe wasn't sure he was that kind of man. He was afraid he would get bored with domestic life. "You'll want someone to talk to, late at night when something's bothering you. You'll need that one day. All men do," Pat explained. Joe wasn't sure of that, either, but he would nod politely, as if he were a believer, too.

Their first call was an open door at the high school gym. There hadn't been too many incidents of vandalism at the school, but last month during the midnight shift someone had spray-painted "Eagles" on the side of one of the buildings. The Eagles were the Crusaders' greatest football adversary, and it was a bitter rivalry. No one had been caught. Joe and Pat headed back toward the school and found the gym door ajar. Once, working with Kathleen, they tried to pull a prank on her at that gym. She got a similar call, although it was Pat's wife who called it in to dispatch, who was also in on the prank. Kathleen arrived and found the gym door open, too. What she didn't know was that Joe and Pat were waiting on the level above the gym floor, armed with water balloons. As she entered the open space, gun drawn and braced over her other arm which held a flashlight, balloons began splashing around her. Every one of them missed. Kathleen yelled at them for ten minutes after she quit laughing, about how she almost shot them, almost shot a hole in the roof of the building. She did not think it was funny, but Joe and Pat had snickered about it for weeks afterward. They both knew, although they never admitted it, that they were lucky something unforgivable didn't happen.

Joe and Pat entered the building in the same manner—guns drawn and ready. A thorough search found no one, and nothing disturbed. They had dispatch call one of the staff members with the appropriate key to relock the door. They wasted thirty minutes waiting for him to arrive and fifteen more minutes listening to him complain about the youth of today. "No respect, not for me, not for you, not for their parents, either. I don't know what we can do to put an end to it, but they'll put an end to me yet, I guarantee." Mitty, the assistant principal, always had something memorable—or unmemorable, depending on the recipient—to offer. Pat and Joe forgot his words as they watched him disappear in the fog that billowed from the exhaust pipe of his '67 Camaro.

Although on duty, Joe and Pat hadn't had the chance to lay their eyes on Steve yet. Joe was apprehensive, but Pat was eager to see the damage. Steve had been answering all the calls during their absence, but at the moment he was up at the PD, filling out some paperwork. They decided to head that way, too. As they walked into the building, Steve met them in the lobby.

"Damn, son, you're scarier than a two-headed frog," said Pat. "I have never seen a bruise like that. Damn, your face looks like a partial eclipse." They all three laughed. Steve's face was black and blue on the left side, from the scalp down to the cheekbone. The color was mottled, giving him an even eerier appearance. Joe was amazed that Steve didn't receive any permanent damage from the blow. And Pat was amazed at the size of his bruise.

"You should see the looks I get. People are more frightened of my face than of my badge. One woman asked me the name of the disease. I told her it was 'fugitive,' and she believed me. I told her that it was contagious, depending on the company she kept. She bought it and took three steps back from me. I nearly died laughing in the car. I can hear her now, telling all her friends about this new disease that discolors the body, called 'fugitive.'"

Steve laughed so hard, he cried. Joe and Pat fell back onto the couch in the waiting area, hysterical. It was the first big laugh they'd shared together, and it seemed to solidify their relationship as a team, officers who worked together and understood one another. They seemed to have bridged the divide that began with Kathleen's death. Joe knew she couldn't be replaced as a partner or a friend, but he realized there was room for others.

Their fun was soon doused by dispatch, calling for both units. "Got a signal twenty-six outside Rock Solid Jewelry. White male, wearing black jeans and black sweatshirt. Caller says he was trying the doors and windows in the back."

"Ten-four. Units nine and fourteen, en route ten fifty-one." The three officers raced out of the PD. Atlas could tell by Pat and Joe's demeanor that something was going on, and he grew agitated. Finding an actual burglary in process was a rare event, but one every officer dreams of. If the subject were trying to break in, they would have a good chance of catching him in the act. A slam dunk legally. Too close to use their sirens, they flew down the road with blue lights on, which they turned off a couple of blocks away from the building.

"Unit fourteen, come back in from the west side. We'll take the east."

"Ten-four. Ten ninety-seven." Steve pulled in quietly, as did Joe a moment later. Steve parked his car a half block away, but Joe's was closer to two. Atlas's barking might scare the burglar off. The three made their way up to the store. Pat was the first to notice him.

"Eleven o'clock, on the corner," he whispered to Joe. Joe notified Steve on the radio of the subject's location.

"Let's watch him — see what he does."

It didn't take but a minute to see him trying to jimmy open the back door with what appeared to be a crowbar. Just as he began to force the door open, Pat stopped him cold.

"Police. Put the crowbar down now." The man froze, the crowbar still perched in his hand. "Drop the crowbar now." Pat's voice was loud this time, and it seemed to snap the man out of his shock. He dropped it but turned to run. Before he took his second step, Joe had him on the ground.

"Didn't know I was there, did you? Get your hands behind your back." Steve cuffed him and checked him for weapons but found none.

"What were you trying to do?" Steve asked.

"What the hell do you think?" The burglar-wannabe was not a stranger to the officers. His name was Michael Evans, a known thief and liar. He had served time for breaking into an elderly woman's home. She had the gumption to pull a gun on him, but Michael overcame her, took the weapon, and fired it at her. Fortunately for him, the bullet missed her, and he served a three-year sentence for aggravated burglary and assault. He had only recently been paroled.

"Another rehabilitated criminal," Joe said to the others.

Joe took the suspect to the PD to complete the necessary paperwork, and Steve transported him to the county jail, about four miles away. When he returned, the three met up at China Moon, an all-you-can-eat Chinese buffet. Steve, still conscious of the bruising on his face, filled his plate quickly and sat down with Pat, who was still full from his dinner at home. Joe soon joined them.

Joe decided to ask the others for input and help in his quest to find Cyrus. He didn't want to make the same mistake Kathleen had and try it on his own. Working together, Joe knew he would stand a better chance of finding what he was looking for.

Just as they were finishing their meals, Joe decided to speak up. "Fellas, I need your help with something." His line of thought was interrupted by the crackling of his radio.

"Unit fourteen, got a signal thirty on Buena Vista. EMS is ten fifty-one."

"Ten-four, unit fourteen, ten fifty-one."

"Same traffic for unit nine."

The three rose from their mostly finished dinner and headed out to the car crash. Pat and Joe directed traffic while Steve took down information for the report. According to a witness, the driver of the Chevy Cavalier ran a red light and struck the Honda Civic. Both cars flipped, and both drivers were injured, but the driver of the Civic was in critical condition according to EMS. Emergency personnel had done all they could once he was extricated from the car. With their reflective vests on, flashlights waving, Joe and Pat kept traffic moving around the debris of broken glass, broken bodies, and broken lives scattered across the intersection. Not wanting to look there anymore, Joe let his eyes wander around the area. He noticed a small white church set back from the road, under a cover of trees. The only way to distinguish it as a church and not a house was the suggestion of a steeple that disappeared between the branches of a huge oak. He never saw the building before and couldn't decide if it was newly built or if he had just overlooked it all these years. After some idle debate, he concluded he had always looked beyond it, but now, for some reason, he couldn't help but look straight at it.

## CHAPTER XIV

Joe never had the chance to discuss his investigation into Kathleen's murder. Not that night, anyway. Working the car crash occupied the balance of Steve's shift, and Pat and Joe had limited time to talk, so the discussion would have to wait. But the delay did not alter Joe's plan to return to Newton in the morning.

Approaching foul weather nearly forced him to reconsider the trip. But since he had nothing more pressing to do that morning, he decided to give it a try. Atlas seemed disappointed not to have the window down. He would look woefully at Joe and then back to the window, imploring with sad brown eyes. Joe was cautious about letting the top down with weather on the way. Once he had had to pull over in heavy rain and lightning to snap the sides of the roof closed, and he had no desire to do it again. Atlas finally gave up and found some contentment in looking through the windshield.

The weather brightened as they made their way north. Joe removed Atlas's badge again, donned a ball cap for himself, and had just enough light to justify wearing sunglasses. Once he reached Newton, he found a road that ran parallel to one of the town's main streets, and parked on the shoulder. He drew out the lead from the backseat. "Here, boy. Where is he? Where is he, boy?"

Atlas was a nondiscriminatory K-9. Unlike a bloodhound, which could distinguish the scent of one person from another, Joe's dog could only follow the strongest scent in a given area, the one the last person had left. But there is only a twenty-minute window in which there would be sufficient scent in the air for him to follow. After those first minutes, a K-9 could only use the decaying ground matter stepped on by the suspect to track him, and that scent could remain for up to eight hours. No, Joe brought Atlas solely for the company. *Let's get him, buddy. Let's get him,* Joe said to himself, though he did not intend to use Atlas to hunt Cyrus's scent.

　　　The two alit from the car with Atlas out in front. His head drew back and forth, not in response to a command, but rather in response to his training, looking for that which had not yet been found. They walked away from town, back in the direction Christina had mentioned to him earlier. Joe sought any sign that would indicate human life in the woods around him. He walked hundreds of yards down trails, looking, searching, but finding nothing. Time was running out for him, and at the last possible moment, after the last possible search, Joe and Atlas headed back to the car. There was too much land to search; Joe became discouraged again. It would be pure luck to come across Cyrus's track, assuming there even was one. "I'm wasting our time, Atlas," he said. "Come on, boy, let's go." But he couldn't. Joe spotted another road perpendicular to their location soon after he drove off. "What the hell," he said, and he turned.

　　　No houses or businesses interrupted the woods on either side, and Joe quickly pulled over to try the impossible once again. "Come on, boy. Last time, I promise. Where is he, buddy? Let's get him." Atlas jumped out on lead again, pulling Joe back and forth along the side of the road as though he had caught someone's scent, when suddenly he stopped, looked up to Joe as if to say something, and then pulled straight back along another beaten trail, deeper into the woods. *Well, I'll be damned,* Joe thought to himself, unable to believe that he'd been so lucky. *But wait...*He grew indecisive. No backup, unknown territory out of his jurisdiction. Not the right way to do it. Not the right way at all. In spite of his emotional will to give chase, he resisted. "Good boy, buddy, good boy." Atlas seemed incredulous, but he obeyed the command and followed Joe to the Jeep. After Joe wrote down enough markers for him to find the easy-to-miss location again, man and beast headed back home to Jackson in a misty rain. It was so fine that Joe couldn't distinguish a single drop, but weighty enough to obscure his view.

This time, the drive passed quickly as Joe planned his next move. He believed that he was closing in. He decided to find the time to let Steve and Pat know what he'd been doing, and ask them to join forces to find Kathleen's killer. He knew he should let the sheriff in on his findings, on Christina's spotting, but even that was uncertain. Anyway, Cyrus was his, and besides, all he had was speculation of the most optimistic kind. The sheriff would think him crazy. No, Joe would do the hunting. The three would return tomorrow with Atlas. They would leave early in the morning and hunt him down. He hoped.

As he neared Jackson, Joe called Jennifer to meet him for lunch, but she already had plans with her coworkers. He wanted to have dinner with her, but knew he would need that time to explain things to Steve and Pat.

"Well, I don't think dinner will work tonight," he said. "How about tomorrow?"

Jennifer agreed, and he promised her a special dinner on his day off. To Jennifer, that meant dressing up and probably heading over to Sebastian's Bay, a beautiful coastal community with wonderful seafood. To Joe, it meant celebrating — he fervently hoped — finding the man who destroyed the other woman he cared about.

Joe drove to a fast-food restaurant to satisfy the voracious appetite he acquired on the way back from Newton. He bought Atlas his own cheeseburger with no bun as a treat for the good work he had done. *Not long now,* Joe thought, *not long before I find you.* He dreaded the start of his shift, wanting instead to return to the only work that mattered right now. But it would give him the chance to talk to the others.

It didn't take long for Joe to find the time once Pat got on duty. Steve had complained about being hungry late in the afternoon, but Joe kept putting him off until Pat joined them.

"Had roast beef, potatoes, and carrots," Pat fairly gloated. "You need to try this marriage thing, Joe," he said as they walked toward Joe's patrol car.

"Yeah. I'll get right on it — one day. Anyway, Steve's starved, and I need to eat, too. You can have some sweet tea at Michelle's, all right?"

"Sure, no problem." Michelle's was a little sandwich shop that served the best key lime pie in town and, some said, in the whole Southeast.

The three met and sat down at the isolated booth Joe requested. They ordered, and as soon as the waitress left the table, Joe began his confession.

"We may not have a lot of time, but I have got to get your help, and you may not like what I'm going to ask of you. Well, you can bet the sheriff in Ellyson knows who Kathleen's killer is." Joe didn't notice Pat's eyes roll. "There's a BOLO out for Cyrus, but he's disappeared. He doesn't have a car as far as we know. No family. No credit cards. No bank account. The shirt off his back—that's all he's got, from what we can tell. But he's a survivalist of sorts. He can hunt and fish and probably live off the land. Probably has a stash of money with him."

"Joe, he's probably long gone," said Pat. "We didn't find Kathleen for days after—well, you know." Pat didn't want to say the word. "He knows people are looking for him. He won't hang around for them to find him." Pat half expected what Joe would say next.

"But maybe he has no place to go. Maybe the land around there is his home. I just have this feeling he stuck around."

"Why's that?" Steve asked just as he took a bite of his ham-and-Swiss on rye.

"I visited a few of the communities around Ellyson, just to see if he might be hiding out. No one really seemed to recognize him from the picture I had, but a waitress from a restaurant in Newton called me on my cell phone and said she spotted him. I drove over there, but I couldn't find him. But yesterday Atlas and I went back, and I found this road I hadn't noticed before. We got out, and Atlas hit on a scent. Of course, it wasn't necessarily Cyrus's, but it was someone's. I started to follow but thought better of it. He knows that land, and I don't. I thought the three of us might go back in the morning and see where it leads us." Joe was grateful he had a plateful of food to look at. He couldn't meet the stare of either man.

"Now, wait a minute. You did all this without letting us in on it?" Pat seemed both angry and somewhat hurt.

"I'm telling you now. Now, what about tomorrow?" With the next day Saturday, Joe knew that

Pat would have no work-related excuse.

"Last I knew, Alabama was just slightly west of our jurisdiction. You're gonna get us all in hot water, Joe." Pat had lost his humor, and Steve was thankful he didn't have to raise his own objections.

"If we find him, we'll back off and call the sheriff. It will be their arrest. We'd just be good citizens, helping them find a bad guy."

"Right, with guns and a police dog. Hey, I know you want this guy—we all do. But I don't want you to jeopardize your job, Joe. I have my own career. I do this for fun. I'm a damn volunteer. But you and Steve, this is your livelihood. I don't want to help you lose it."

"Pat, you've been my partner of sorts for years now. I trust you, and I thought you trusted me. I have to do this, and I need your help. I shouldn't have to say any more. I shouldn't." Joe slammed down his drink, bouncing iced tea all over his plate.

Both Pat and Steve were mute as they tried to finish their lunch. Joe thought Steve's silence was his tacit disapproval. Finally Pat spoke up. "You're right. We should be there for each other. But I will do no more than help you find him. After that, I'm out of there, and you're on your own."

"I'll be right there with you, Pat. I'm not going to do anything stupid. What about you, Steve? Are you in?"

"I'm in, Joe. Don't get us fired, though."

"I won't. Thanks. I really mean it." Joe was relieved, but also worried. Each man considered the possibilities, and none of them finished his meal.

By the end of their shift, Joe had devised a game plan. "Dress in jeans and work boots. Bring binoculars. We'll say we're tracking muskrat habitat in Alabama or something like that. But we won't be hunters, just observers. I'll even bring a camera." They agreed to meet at Joe's apartment at seven-thirty so they could be in Newton by ten.

After a restless night's sleep, Joe woke up and turned to look at Kathleen's dresser. He said, "I'm doing what I can, Kathleen. I'll find him, I promise." He showered, dressed, and headed out to the Jackson Bakery for some freshly made honey buns. It was the least he could do for Pat and Steve. Soon after he returned, the two arrived. No one had to mention it, but each man was armed with a gun strapped to his ankle holster. Joe removed Atlas's badge once again, and the foursome left in Joe's Jeep to find Kathleen's killer.

Steve was unusually talkative during the drive, but none of his conversation concerned the job that awaited them. He had begun his law enforcement career in corrections. He worked the evening shift at the prison so that he could take classes at the local college during the day. In three years of heavy loads, Steve finished his degree in law enforcement, with a minor in political science. "I'd like to be chief one day, Joe, and you'd make a damn good sergeant."

"Ha-ha. You'll be *my* sergeant, Steve."

"What about me, fellas? What will my title be?" Pat asked, feigning hurt feelings.

"Chief of the part-timers, Pat. Volunteer of the year." Joe appreciated their good humor.

Joe had no trouble finding the spot Atlas and he had marked the day before. Armed with binoculars, a camera, and hidden weapons, the four left the comfort of the Jeep. There was little breeze and no clouds—the perfect kind of day to follow a track, assuming one had been left recently. Before Joe could contemplate giving Atlas a command to search, the dog grew agitated. And once again Atlas, on lead, set his course down the exposed trail that led into a dense forest of pines and water oaks. The hunt was on. And just as quickly, it was off.

In less than five minutes, Atlas lost the track. According to Joe, there were only a couple of explanations: the person had either vanished into thin air, which was impossible, or, more likely had backtracked down the trail to the road, — assuming, of course, that Atlas was ever following Cyrus's scent to begin with. The three men and one dog studied the ground, but the earth was covered with too many leaves and other natural debris for them to see any marks that anything or anyone might have left. There was nothing to see, nothing to track, and nothing more to do. Embarrassed and apologetic, Joe drove the men back to Jackson.

"I blew it. I'm sorry, fellas. A damn wild-goose chase, and I dragged you all along."

Yet neither man faulted Joe. "It looked good from the road, and you were right not to follow that trail on your own. Don't worry about it. Police work isn't always smooth, right?" Pat tried to make light of the situation. "Maybe the bastard suffered from spontaneous combustion, and we just walked over his grave. Who knows? Maybe he was there. We'll have other chances."

"Next time I'll be more sure of myself before I drag them along," Joe thought to himself. He then realized that maybe that was how Kathleen felt. Maybe Kathleen wasn't sure of what she believed and was looking for confirmation before she asked for help. That made sense to Joe, and he was desperately looking for some sense in all this. That made perfect sense. She hadn't eliminated her partner from what she was doing;

she just wanted to convince herself first. How could he blame her?

After apologizing again for wasting their Saturday morning, Joe felt certain that Pat and Steve left with no misgivings. Atlas was in need of a bath, so Joe threw on his old shorts and turned on the hose. Atlas loved getting bathed. He loved the cool water massaging between his muscular shoulders and even seemed to like the scent of the shampoo Joe used. And he especially liked nailing Joe with the final shake-off. As Joe dried Atlas's legs, he noticed an unfamiliar car drive into the complex. It parked quickly, and Joe didn't get a look at the driver. He thought no more of it. He had no way of knowing Cyrus was behind the wheel.

## PART III

## CHAPTER I

Not long after Joe first nosed around Newton, Cyrus stopped in a gas station - bait shop to get a few supplies. After making sure no one was around, he slipped inside. Cyrus caught a glimpse of himself in the reflection of the store window. Unshaven and unwashed, he looked like some swamp creature. But Peter, one of the twins, immediately recognized him and had something to tell.

"Cyrus, someone's been looking for you. I didn't get his name when he was here, but he said someone left you some land or money or something, and he was trying to find you to give it to. I didn't believe him. He drove off in a Jeep with a Florida tag, and I wrote down the number." Peter paused for some kind of response, but Cyrus only stared. "I called a deputy friend of mine in Alopsa, and he told me the car belonged to Joe Carpenter from Jackson, Florida. Here's the address on his registration. Thought you might want to know." Peter and Mark had known Cyrus since elementary school. They weren't close — no one was ever close to Cyrus — but they had a healthy respect based mostly on their fear of him. Cyrus had earned that reverence by winning after-school fights in which the loser often had to be carried off. Peter had been one of those boys, and he made a point of doing all he could for Cyrus merely for the sake of self-preservation. They had known about the murder in Ellyson and knew that Cyrus lived there, but they thought it best not to put two and two together—at least not to Cyrus.

"Much obliged for the information. Let's just keep it between us, okay?" Cyrus made his wishes clear.

"No problem, Cyrus, none at all. What can we get you today?" Peter was ready to change the subject of their conversation.

"Couple of loaves of bread, some of those cheese crackers, and some toilet paper. That should hold me a while. Say, you don't have any pickles, do you?"

"Sour dills only. We don't stock those sweet things."

"Good. Sour's the only kind I like."

Cyrus paid cash for his small cache of goods. He walked out of the store, and neither twin tried to see where he went. Better not to know, they thought.

"Sour's about right," mumbled Peter.

"What do you mean?" asked Mark, not really interested in pickles at the moment.

"Cyrus's life, I mean. No dad around, a mother who might as well been gone, having to take care of her so many years. I'll bet he never heard nothing like 'thank you' from her, neither." Peter shook his head. "Yeah, nothin' but sour."

Cyrus didn't go too far, just around the corner to a pay phone. He called Jackson information for the police department's number. Once he'd loaded up the slot with coins, he called the station. Deborah answered.

"Yes, ma'am. Is there a Joe Carpenter working today?" Cyrus disguised his voice as best he could in case he was being recorded.

"No, he's off today. Did you want to leave a message?"

"No, that's okay. When does he work again?"

"Not until Monday. Evening shift."

"I'll try him then." Cyrus learned what he suspected. He pulled the shiny badge he had taken from Kathleen's car. He now knew Joe was the law, and he figured he'd have to hunt him down. Cyrus was not going to be put in any kind of cage, *no way in hell*, but to keep his freedom, he would require a car. Cyrus sneaked back around the corner and into the twins' station again. They were frightened at his reappearance.

"I need a car, maybe for a week or more. You know where I might find one that won't be missed?"

The twins didn't want to know its purpose. Peter spoke up first. "Yeah, my uncle has an old Plymouth. He had a stroke and don't drive now. I'll tell him I'm lending it to an old school buddy. He won't mind. I'm sure of it." Cyrus slowly nodded at the news, and Peter picked up the phone to make the call. Mark shuffled his feet, not wanting to cross Cyrus but not wanting to help him either. Their uncle didn't hesitate to help the twins' friend. Peter and Cyrus left in Peter's Buick and headed up the road.

"I don't have to meet your uncle, do I?" Cyrus asked, but Peter already knew the answer.

"Nah, I'll make up some excuse. Don't worry about it, Cyrus. I'll take care of it."

Within five minutes of pulling into the uncle's driveway, Peter had secured the keys to the car. "Told you it wasn't no problem. She hasn't been driven much lately—prob'ly needs gas and all, but she purrs just like a little kitten. Here's the keys. If you have any problems, you know where to find me." Peter had a little difficulty in getting his uncle to hand his car over to someone he'd never met, but Peter assured him that his friend was good and, but for a severe shyness around strangers, would have come in to thank him.

"I owe you, Peter," Cyrus said, and Peter knew that was money he could take to the bank.

Cyrus checked the oil under the hood. It was full but a little dirty. The engine turned over the first time, but there was less than a quarter tank of gas, so Cyrus eased on back to the twins' station, filled up, then stopped by his lean-to in the woods on the way to Jackson.

Realizing he might attract too much attention looking the way he did, he stopped off at a motel on the outskirts of town. At the thrift store next door he bought some cleaner-looking clothes, then checked in to get himself cleaned up. He didn't shave his beard or mustache, however, hoping the facial hair would alter his appearance some. He searched for and found a phone book stuck in the nightstand drawer and looked up Joe's name. When he found no listing, it occurred to Cyrus that Joe may live in another nearby city. Not prepared to deal with such possibilities, he decided that the bed, after these weeks of sleeping on the ground, looked too inviting, and he took a nap that lasted until dinnertime. He got a bite to eat at the diner next door and decided to look around the town. When he felt comfortable with the layout of the area, he would then set out to find Joe, the only person he saw standing in the way of his future. Not that Cyrus had any grand plan for his life, but Joe stood in the way of his freedom, and Cyrus, like many animals, wouldn't survive long in a pen.

Cyrus didn't like to think too much and felt more comfortable reacting than acting. That was how it had been growing up with his mother. He had always reacted to their environment: hunted for food when the stockpile was low, fed the chickens when they came close to the house, ducked when his mother swung the broom his way. Not that his mother beat him — she wasn't strong or quick enough — but Cyrus had to be on the lookout. His life was spent responding to what happened around him, but things were different now. Cyrus had to plan his attack.

Jackson had a lot more to offer than Ellyson, not that Cyrus really cared. He drove past malls and subdivisions, multi-storied buildings and schools. There were several motels, most nicer looking than the one where he was holed up, but he wasn't much for appearances. He noticed that Jackson had a Chinese restaurant, a treat he didn't often get, and he decided to try it out during his stay. He drove up and down the main avenues, familiarizing himself with street names and landmarks, and finally he turned back toward the police station.

After parking in the lot of what appeared to be an abandoned building, Cyrus walked around the corner to a long-limbed oak tree that would shield his body from view of the station's front door, and he settled down to watch. He watched the officers' habits: their comings and goings, how and where they parked, and whether they locked their patrol cars. He watched how they walked and talked with one another. He was getting to know the enemy, and his watch became a vigil. After hours of reconnaissance and much mental note taking, Cyrus called it a night and headed back to the motel, where he slept a luxurious nine hours without ever waking.

After a full breakfast of eggs, bacon, grits, and biscuits at the diner, Cyrus took care of some basic housekeeping back in his room. He cleaned his gun — actually Kathleen's .40–caliber Glock , but it belonged to him now, he told himself. He loved the feel of gun oil slipping through his fingers, and the motion of pushing the bore brush along the barrel, through the bore and out the muzzle. He wiped down every crevice and worked the action satisfied that the tool would function perfectly. He also counted out his money. Cyrus had just over $32,000 in cash, all stuffed into an old army duffel bag — enough money to cover his hunt and his escape. Finally, he sorted the few personal effects he had: a picture of his mother, unsmiling as she usually was, a picture bent at every edge and creased everywhere in between; a driver's license, so worn the laminate had mostly worn off leaving only the card itself; a hunting license, long since expired; and finally, a police badge, shiny, smooth, and cold.

Now he was looking for a different badge, but the problem was, he didn't know the face that went with it. All he knew about Joe was that he was a cop with black or dark brown hair, according to the twins, and that he drove a Jeep.

Referring to the address Peter gave him, Cyrus found the apartment complex easily and drove down the driveway that led to a series of buildings, looking for apartment 1701. Before he found what he sought, he caught a glimpse of a man and a dog standing next to a Jeep. Uncertain whether it was Joe, he pulled in the closest parking space. Through his rearview mirror, he watched them both enter unit 1701. He had found his man. He now knew what Joe looked like, knew what his patrol car, a K-9 unit, looked like, and what his Jeep looked like. Cyrus was surprised to learn that Joe had a dog, not that it mattered greatly, but it was just another thing to consider. He found what he came for, and for Cyrus, his day was done. He had tomorrow to look forward to.

In the meantime, Cyrus craved some Chinese food from the restaurant he noticed the night before. From a service station phone booth he placed a to-go order: cashew chicken, sweet-and-sour chicken, three egg rolls, fried rice, and wontons — afraid to spend too much time in any one public place in the heart of Jackson. He darted in and out of China Moon with his hoard, keeping his cap pulled low. Back at the motel, he dined in style, in front of the TV, sitting on a double bed, with the air-conditioning on high. He would have to wait one more day before he could meet Joe in person. Cyrus was ready, and now he was content.

# CHAPTER II

Joe wasn't ready to get out of bed, even though the alarm screamed at him to wake up. He had been deep in a dream that he couldn't quite remember, except that it seemed he could get nowhere, as if he were caught in quicksand. *It's just a damn dream.* He had only set the alarm because he needed to run errands, lots of them, which he had neglected over the past couple of weeks. His uniforms needed dry cleaning, he needed to go to the bank, he had bills to pay and an empty refrigerator to fill, and he had to do it all before his lunch with Jennifer before work. He also felt like going for a run. It had been nearly a month since he last ran. Joe tried to make running a habit, not necessarily a daily one, but he liked to hit it frequently after spending so many hours sitting in his patrol car.

At first his legs felt strong and powerful, but his recent lack of aerobic activity caught up to him just short of the first mile. He had been able to run over four. Unable to continue, or perhaps just unwilling, Joe walked halfway back to the apartment and then forced himself to run the final leg disappointed that he had lost his stamina both physically and mentally. He had quit, and he hated a quitter.

He tried to shake off the feeling as he showered, dressed, and ran his errands. He looked forward to seeing Jennifer, and arrived at La Hacienda ten minutes early to ensure they would have a table. Jennifer walked in right on time.

"Hi, honey, how are you?" Jennifer wanted to say more, like perhaps "I miss you," but something stopped her.

"Better now. I like that dress. Is it new?" Joe never asked her about her clothes.

"No, I just haven't worn it that much." She didn't tell Joe that her worrying about him had helped her lose five pounds, which made more of her wardrobe available for wear.

They ordered and exchanged small talk. Joe couldn't understand it. Nothing felt comfortable, and he blamed it on the letdown he felt after dragging Steve and Pat on his worthless jaunt to Newton. He had to put Cyrus out of his life, or he wouldn't be able to live it.

The couple finished their meal, and Joe escorted Jennifer to her car. Leaning into the open door, he said, "I know I'm not myself. I will be again, Jennifer. Just hang in there, okay?"

"You know I will," she said. "I wish you could talk to me more, that's all. I wish you could share more, Joe. It would probably help us both."

He could say little more than "I know...I know."

Frustrated by all that had happened in the past thirty-six hours, Joe began his shift in a less-than-pleasant humor. Cyrus had no way of knowing this, however, watching from his perch across the street.

Wendy read Joe's mood the moment she saw him. "How was your weekend?" It was all she could think to say. Atlas lumbered up to her for his afternoon petting.

"It's over. Anything going on here?" Joe glanced through the past few days of calls in the pass-down. He noted that the midnight shift had made two arrests, one for a domestic and one for a DUI.

"Not really. Seems pretty quiet."

Joe checked his mailbox for messages and mail. He had two subpoenas for old cases and no messages. Steve walked up.

"Hey, Joe, Megan invited us to eat over at her place tonight. She's making a pot of chili, so it doesn't matter when we eat."

"Sounds good. Maybe we'll get lucky and not have to wolf down our dinner for a change." Truth was, sometimes they didn't have time to eat at all.

Steve and Joe met at the fueling station. Cyrus was there, too, behind them, watching from his parked car adjacent to the empty lot. Just as Joe was about to leave and resume his walk-and-talks, Wendy radioed him.

"Unit nine, need a welfare check at 1818 Mencken Street. Call me on the eight hundred." The 800 request always meant there was information not to be publicized over the airways.

"Go ahead, Wendy," he said once he picked up the handheld.

"Seems the owner of the house threatened suicide a couple of weeks ago to some of his church people. He didn't show up for a counseling class, so they went by his house. His car's there, lights are on, and the TV's blasting, but no one will answer the door."

Joe did not like the sound of that. "Ten-four," he replied. Joe never had dealings with the man, so he didn't really know what to expect, but he would know something shortly. He drove up and found a small crowd outside the front door of Justin Wallin's house.

"Afternoon, folks. What can you tell me?"

One man spoke up. "I'm Reverend Alan Griffin. Justin attends our church. He's been having a hard time lately, and we've tried to be there for him, but now I'm afraid we're too late. He mentioned suicide a few times. I know he's in there, but he won't answer the door. I have a bad feeling…" The man was noticeably distraught.

"When's the last time you saw him?" Joe started jotting notes on his spiral pad.

"Two days ago. At church."

"How long have you been here?" Joe asked, hoping it was only minutes.

"About half an hour."

"Okay, I'm going to check around the house. I ask that you stay back from it, okay? Let me do my job. By the way, does he have any weapons that you know of?"

The minister shrugged. "I don't really know," he said.

Joe walked the perimeter of the house, looking in windows and trying to open them. He could see nothing behind the drawn blinds. The two doors were locked, and Joe's knocks remained unanswered. But Joe did find access. One of the front windows was partially broken — he could get inside there.

"Unit fourteen, what's your twenty?" Joe thought it prudent to get backup just in case.

"Just around the corner from you."

"Ten-four. Ease on by."

"Ten-four."

Joe explained the situation to him when he arrived, and Steve, too, was somewhat concerned.

"Steve, let's break out the rest of that window. I'll climb in and open the door for you." He knew that entering a home under such circumstances was a dangerous thing. If Justin was just asleep, once he heard his front window breaking, he could rightly defend himself against the intruder. He could be armed. Or if he was suicidal, he might just be waiting for such a standoff, hoping he could force the police officer to be the trigger man. In all cases, entering a home like this was risky, and both men knew it. Nevertheless, they had to get in, and after talking to the churchgoers, Joe determined that there was no family member who might be of help. Phone calls to the house echoed through the breach.

Joe withdrew his expandable baton from his gun belt. In the event Justin was inside and still alive, Joe thought it sensible to announce his entrance. "Justin, it's Officer Carpenter with the Jackson Police. I'm coming in to talk to you, okay? Justin?" No new sounds issued from the house. Using the baton's tip, Joe broke out the remaining glass while he stood at an angle away from the window, careful so that if Justin had a gun, the bullet might miss him. Before he penetrated the window frame, both he and Steve listened, but neither could distinguish anything meaningful. Cyrus listened, too, only fifteen yards from the house, hidden behind some tall azaleas, hoping that Justin would do the job for him, and then hoping that he wouldn't. Cyrus wanted the pleasure of meeting Joe himself, and the pleasure of telling him good-bye.

The window was about three feet off the ground, so Joe had to lift himself up to the sash, and with Steve's help, he got himself over the sill. Moving quickly inside, Joe glanced around the living room as he crouched on the hardwood floor. Nothing moved, so he crept to the front door, unlocked the deadbolt, and let Steve in. Still no movement. The two men split up—Joe to the rooms on the right and Steve to the left. They both sensed death in that house, but it was Joe who found it—in the bedroom, lying on the bed, eyes wide open, head partially blown away.

"Steve, he's here." Joe felt his heart racing at the

sight of all the blood on the bed and the floor below it. He couldn't help but think of Kathleen and her lifeless body.

"Damn it...*Damn it.*" Steve could think of nothing more to say.

Joe did what he should instinctively, not because he believed there was any hope. He felt for a pulse on the other side of the body, the one that looked whole except for a small entrance wound near the temple. There was no life. He called EMS to pronounce the time of death.

"Unit nine, Jackson, we have an apparent signal thirty-three. Contact the investigator on duty."

"Ten-four, unit nine. Stand by." Wendy could remember only one real suicide in Jackson since she began working there four years ago. Several lonely people had tried, but only one had succeeded. She called Tony McCoy at home, and he answered on the second ring.

"Tony? We've—"

"I know," he said, cutting her off. "I heard it on the scanner. What's the location?" Tony was the most senior investigator at the department, but even he had never worked a suicide.

Wendy gave Tony the information and relayed to Joe that he was on his way. She also told him that Pat wouldn't be able to work with him—said he had a family obligation.

"Just as well," said Joe.

In the meantime, Joe and Steve left the house to retrieve crime scene tape and give some answers to the crowd outside. Cyrus watched the two officers walk out.

"Folks, we're going to need you to leave the area after we get a little information." Joe didn't want to explain what had happened, but he knew that would be difficult.

The minister spoke up first. "Is he in there?" He was trying to read their faces and was afraid he saw the answer.

"He's dead, isn't he?" asked another.

"I know you're worried about Justin. But the best way to help him is to cooperate with us. There's nothing more you can do for him, understand?" Joe was sure they could read between the lines.

Steve interviewed them all and got their basic information while Joe marked off the exterior of the house with crime scene tape. Department policy was to treat every death as a homicide, at least in the beginning, until the evidence said otherwise. By the time Joe finished, Tony drove up to the house.

Tony spoke briefly with Steve and the people he had interviewed, and then asked them to leave. He walked around the exterior of the house, checking doors and windows just as Steve and Joe had done. Only then did he enter, along with the officers who had discovered Justin. Cyrus watched all this with some degree of boredom and decided Joe would be occupied for some time, longer than he wanted to wait, so he headed back to China Moon for an order to go. He would find Joe again tomorrow.

Tony took notes every step along the way to Justin's body. He noted the window that Joe had broken out and crawled through. He jotted down that according to the officers, the house was locked from the inside. He observed that the television was on in the living room and the volume turned up loud. He turned it off.

Justin's self-created crypt merited a clean sheet of paper. The light was on, and the blood on the hardwood floor was tacky and almost dry. Justin lay on his back. It appeared that he had clinched his left hand, the hand not holding the gun, and held the fist up to his face next to the ear, as he pulled the trigger, because a graze wound ran along the third knuckle. There was, of course, an exit wound on the left side of his head, and below that, small pieces of skull and brain matter scattered on the pillow, bed, floor, and wall. Tony made his notes and took telling photographs, and Joe and Steve watched as the life of a man was reduced to a couple of pages in a spiral notebook and a handful of two-dimensional impressions.

The three looked for a note Justin might have left, something that would give them some inkling of why he did this to himself, but they found nothing. Joe did, however, find the receipt for the gun and bullets in a plain brown paper bag. Justin had purchased the gun four days ago and waited the requisite three days to pick it up. The waiting period hadn't made a difference this time. The weapon lay still partially gripped in Justin's limp hand. Tony took a pair of latex gloves from his pocket, pulled them on, and with Steve and Joe unable to do more than watch, released each finger from the grip. Finally he removed the means of self-destruction from the man who had given up. Joe didn't have time then to question why. Tony laid the gun on the floor, just below the hand that had held it last.

Tony called the chief, just to assure him it was indeed a suicide and then called the medical examiner to pick up the body. The entire process, from finding Justin to getting him out of his home, took almost four hours. Neither Steve nor Joe realized how spent they were until they finally got to sit down. The drive back to the PD was brief, and each wanted more time to contemplate what they had witnessed tonight. But they had paperwork to complete first; there would be time for questioning later.

The melancholy mood in the PD was palpable even before Joe and Steve arrived. Kathleen's murder, Steve's injury and now the suicide, all within a span of weeks, were strange at best and ominous at worst. Everyone in the department felt some degree of nervousness, wondering what would happen next and whom it would involve. Joe, upon reflection, began to think of himself as a sort of grim reaper. Only he had seen both dead bodies, both with part of the head removed, both isolated, both alone. And when he found Steve, he, too, was alone and broken. Even though Justin was a stranger, Joe felt an odd sympathy for him, for the friends he probably had but didn't trust enough to share whatever pain he was going through. He thought about the preacher and his bunch who tried to reach out but were rebuffed. He thought of Kathleen and how, because she placed all her trust in herself alone, she was now lost forever. All Joe's thinking brought him back to Steve and Pat and Jennifer, the people in his life he cared about, and who, he believed, cared about him, too. He hadn't really ever let them into his life, hadn't really trusted his urge to share with them, and now, if he didn't change, he could end up just like Kathleen or Justin. Joe finished his work, finished his shift, and started his life.

## CHAPTER III

The sun had just risen above the tops of the pines, and the day was already warm and bright. Joe ran the streets of Jackson, shirtless, enjoying the feel of the breeze against his skin. Even though he was out of the habit of running, today he felt light on the pavement. His arms were relaxed, his mind at ease as he drifted down streets and around buildings. His sunglasses shielded him from the intensity of the day but nothing could defend him from the rising heat. He enjoyed feeling the perspiration spill off his body, as if it were a sort of catharsis exorcising all the bad he had seen lately. It had begun last night, when he called Jennifer at the end of his shift and asked if he could stop by. The late-night "hello" turned into a four-hour conversation. Joe still liked what he saw in Jennifer, and it was pretty clear that she felt the same way. He was still working on the "brutally honest" thing, but it didn't come to him by nature. It was a skill he would have to learn.

Turning back toward his apartment, he noticed cars as they passed, saw a few faces he recognized. Sometimes he thought he saw Kathleen driving, and now Justin, but he knew it was just memories he couldn't yet drive away.

He looked forward to getting back to work—real police work, arresting the real criminals—and he spent some extra time playing with his ally, Atlas, who looked a little sad and neglected lately. Man and dog played an extended game of tug-of-war all over the narrow yard before Joe showered and changed.

Cyrus watched everything. He had driven up to Joe's apartment first thing in the morning just to watch Joe's activity. After Joe ran out of the complex, Cyrus followed at a distance, watching the man he had grown to hate. He hated that Joe was a cop, hated that he drove a Jeep, hated that he had the physique of a runner. He even hated Joe's German shepherd. Cyrus resented anyone who had anything, and above all hated anyone who would try to take what little he had away. He hadn't stood for it with Emma Johnson, he didn't stand for it with her granddaughter, Kathleen, and he wasn't about to stand for it with Joe.

Two things mattered most in killing Joe: it had to happen face-to-face, and Joe must be on duty. That way he could see the fear in Joe's eyes, could strip away another badge, and the police would suspect one of the local ne'er-do-wells and not him. So Cyrus would bide his time, watch Joe from a distance, and make his move when no one else was around. Whether it was today or next week mattered little to Cyrus—he had only time to lose and no better place to spend it. He became a regular at China Moon.

Even though Joe had accepted the events that had rocked him so strongly, Steve hadn't. Joe could see it in his face right away.

"Hey, Steve, rough night, huh? We can't let it get to us, though, you know? People make bad decisions every day. I'm trying to limit mine, keep them in the single digits every day." His hokey attempt to make Steve laugh wasn't working.

Steve shook his head. "The picture of him in my mind won't go away. It doesn't even seem real. Weird, I guess, that a cop would be bothered by that, and I don't like to admit it anyway, but I am. I guess it's because I've never seen a suicide before. Probably won't be my last, huh?" Steve seemed ashamed at this admission.

Joe understood. "It bothered me, too, buddy, until I realized that maybe I was *supposed* to see Justin, to see what could happen if I tried to handle life on my own. I could be Justin one day—we all could be if we take life too seriously, if we don't let people into our worlds. Justin decided to go solo, and I decided last night that I want a few copilots in my life, some people I can really trust. I'm telling you this, I told Jennifer that last night, and I'll tell Pat if he comes out tonight. And don't think this isn't hard for me, because it damn sure is." Joe was beginning to feel foolish because Steve hadn't acknowledged any of what Joe said for what seemed like a long time now.

Finally Steve responded. "Man, I know what you're saying. I don't want to go there, either. We're a family, I guess, one I trust my life with."

They shook hands, discussed some current cases, and got to work, knowing that the brief moment of shared vulnerability between the two men brought them closer, though neither would speak of it again.

Joe and Steve worked together most of the afternoon. At the chief's request, they ran radar along a couple of residential streets. Neither enjoyed the work particularly, but it was a necessary evil in police work, and the chief wanted it. After citing four cars in an hour, they decided to take a break and cruise around the area.

Cyrus couldn't find a hidden vantage point where he might watch them work. He was brazen enough to drive by them once, but then, realizing he was taking too big a chance, he parked up the street, just close enough to see Joe's back bumper. He was getting bored, but he was on the trail now and wasn't about to slack off. He was pleased to see Joe finally drive off, but he drove off the other way. Cyrus had difficulty turning around on the busy street and lost his prey, but only temporarily.

Back in the quiet of his car, Joe gave voice to his obsession with Cyrus. "I know you're out there, you bastard. I'll get you, I promise." He breathed deeply and tried to focus on the task ahead of him.

Joe and Steve patrolled the string of lower-end apartments on the west side of town. Activity seemed minimal. They headed back toward the PD at Wendy's request. She needed a cheeseburger, and Pat had called to say he was on his way.

By the time they arrived, Pat was already there, feeling a little disjointed because he had missed the previous night. He was reading the pass-down as the two men and one dog walked in.

"Hey, Pat. Ready to do some real work tonight?"

Pat immediately noticed the change in Joe. Wendy had told him of the suicide Joe worked the night before. "You bet," he said. "Was last night bad?"

"Guess it could have been worse." Joe was trying out his blunt honesty again. "The whole thing was pretty awful. Brain matter and skull and blood speckled all over the room. It got me to thinking about my life. I'm glad I have a few good friends."

Although neither had said so before, Pat felt the same way about Joe, but he was surprised at Joe's admission. "Damn," he replied, "I figured sooner or later you'd learn what was important. Back at you."

They didn't have to say much to communicate. Joe filled Pat in on the events of the day, and together they set off to do the job they both loved so much.

And outside, Cyrus waited to do the job he knew

would bring him the greatest pleasure. Pat's arrival might make the job more difficult, but Cyrus liked a challenge. He would just have to wait for them to get separated. Wendy gave the officers their first call as they were leaving the PD. It was the worst kind: a domestic. Neighbors in the apartment building heard breaking glass and screaming. The ruckus had been going on for the past thirty minutes and seemed to be getting worse. The couple had recently moved in, but that was about all anyone knew.

Whenever there appears to be imminent danger to a person, the police get there as quickly as they can sometimes without using lights and sirens. But the speed and noise of the accelerating engine were enough to thrust Atlas into bark mode, hopeful that he would have something important to do. Steve, too, was speeding to the scene. The two cars arrived at nearly the same time. No noise could be heard from the street.

Cyrus couldn't follow at Joe's speed without drawing attention to himself, so he drove in their general direction, hoping he would catch sight of their cars at some point. It took a while, but he found them and watched from a distance.

As the three officers neared the apartment, they could distinguish muffled crying just on the other side of the front door. The lights were on, and through the thin muslin curtains they could see a figure moving inside. Steve knocked on the door with the back of his flashlight.

"Police. Open up!"

"Who the hell called you?" asked the slurring male voice from within.

"Open this door now!"

"Hold your damn horses. Move, Jessie!" She was still crying.

The three officers drew back just a little from the door, just in case the man was armed. They heard the deadbolt slide and watched the knob turn. Just as the man cracked open the door, Joe forced his Maglite into the gap.

"Need you to step out here, sir. Now!" Something in Joe's tone forced the man to follow his directions. Once outside, Joe patted him down for weapons but found nothing. Pat stayed with Joe while Steve went inside to check on the woman.

He was sickened by what he saw. She lay in a fetal position by the door. Her left cheek was swollen, and a small break in the skin there was bleeding slightly. Her neck was red, and there were visible finger impressions there. Mascara had run down her face, chased by her tears, giving her an even more pitiful appearance.

"Ma'am, are you okay?"

Her response was only to cry louder. Steve offered his hand to help her up, but she flinched as it came toward her.

"I'm not going to hurt you. I'm the police. I'm here to protect you. Let's get you over to the couch, okay? You'll be more comfortable." This time she let him help her. Pat walked in, took one look at the woman, and walked out with handcuffs drawn.

"Who did this to you?" She pointed out the door.

"What's his name? Is he your husband?" He didn't notice a wedding band.

Between sobs she was able to cough out, "Ricky," and "yes."

After some cajoling, the wife, Flora, told Steve that when she came home from work, Ricky was already drunk. She was a half hour late, trying to get in some overtime, and he accused her of fooling around. It was a story Steve had heard too many times before; only the names changed. He lectured her on how she didn't deserve to be treated this way and that she had the opportunity to leave him. She gave him all the answers he wanted, but he doubted that she would do anything to help herself. So few did, and he had real trouble understanding why. But by Florida law, Flora didn't have to file a complaint; the State mandates that the officers do it. Ricky was going to jail, and she had twenty-four hours to make some changes. Steve completed all the required forms for a domestic violence incident and gave her pamphlets about abuse, but he feared that it fell on indifferent ears.

Because the backseat of Joe's car was not designed for human transport, Steve put Ricky in the back of his patrol car to transfer him to the county jail and complete the arrest report there. They headed off as Joe and Pat headed to another call, this time for a signal twenty-six: suspicious person.

"Black male, headed east on the railroad tracks just past the old train station. Caller states he's throwing rocks into the street at cars. He's wearing blue jeans and a dark shirt."

"Ten-four. Be ten fifty-one." Joe liked busy nights, but he hated men who got a thrill from hurting women.

There was no easy access to the railroad right-of-way by car, so they parked three blocks east of the suspect's last known location and walked west. Their flashlights showed them nothing at all on the tracks, but hiding places abounded on either side. The north side was little more than a drop-off into a gully, with thick woods just beyond that, and the south side was occupied by fenceless homes and driveways that led to the road.

Joe and Pat walked every block but could find nothing but a stray dog, wandering as they were.

Cyrus drove past Joe's patrol car but couldn't find an inconspicuous place to park. He didn't know what they were doing or how long they would be gone, and he was growing hungry. But with the other officer gone, he had a better chance of getting Joe alone. Cyrus noticed the two flashlight beams flicking about between two houses and realized he just might get his chance.

"Pat, let's head back to the car and drive down toward the park. Maybe he made it there already."

"Yeah, I don't think he's here. Let's go." The two men walked back to the car and drove a short distance. They made their way back on foot, staying close to the railroad, no flashlights this time, listening and watching. After a minute or two of this, a figure emerged from beside one of the houses and turned to walk in their direction. Not wanting to spook him into running, they held their position until he was a mere couple of feet away. Joe stepped out from behind the tree.

"Police. I need to talk to you." Joe almost laughed as he watched the man jump, surprised by the officer's appearance.

"What the hell you want? I'm not bothering you or nobody." He didn't notice Pat coming up behind him.

"We've got a report of someone who matches your description throwing rocks from these tracks at cars over there. What's up with that, man?"

"Ah, damn. I threw one stupid rock and someone called about it? I wasn't trying to hit a car. I was just throwing a rock—you know, just being me." Joe and Pat knew Marcus; they had had dealings with him before. He wasn't really a troublemaker, although it always seemed to follow him.

"Well, don't do it again, got it, Marcus? You don't want me coming back out here again, do you?"

"No, man. I'll be more careful."

"Take it easy, Marcus."

Cyrus crept back toward the street and to his car. Only Marcus left the area content. Joe and Pat wanted another arrest; Cyrus wanted Joe. All three would have to wait.

Steve called Joe on the 800. "Hey, I'm starved. You guys up for getting a bite somewhere?"

"You bet. How about pizza for a change?"

"Sounds good. Meet you there in ten."

Estelle's was Jackson's only Italian restaurant. They served little more than lasagna, spaghetti, and wonderful pizza, but they never scrimped on the toppings. Pat sat by the window, not that there was much to look at in the alleyway, but he was more comfortable in a position where he could watch what was coming. Most of their conversation revolved around wives and girlfriends—what made them happy and what ticked them off. Basically, their women were pretty much the same but in very different ways, they concluded, and that was just fine with everyone.

Unexpectedly, the trio got to eat their meal in peace—no calls during the entire forty-five minutes. Cyrus grew angry at the time he was wasting. He watched them eat and drink and laugh as he stood alone in the darkness of the alley, waiting for the situation to change. Cyrus was growing impatient, which was unusual for him because he had never been in a hurry to do anything. Another person was in control of his life, and that, too, had never happened since his mother died. *Gracie—funny name for a woman who was about as graceful as a newborn calf and half as pretty,* Cyrus thought to himself. He didn't miss her—wasn't sure whether he had ever loved her, and certain she had never wanted his love. Gracie had been cold-hearted to kin and strangers alike. "Nobody misses her," he whispered in the empty alleyway.

The three officers left the restaurant "fat and sassy," as Pat put it, and headed for some strip malls to check on the businesses there. Pat and Joe drove up on some skateboarders making the most of the empty sidewalk to get a little practice in, although signs were clearly posted that they weren't allowed to pursue their sport in that area. Steve drove on to the next center, a block away, to check on doors and windows there.

Joe stepped out of the car first to admonish the board riders. "Guys, you see the sign. I know you all read, so take your gear somewhere else." The teenagers knew it was coming when they saw the patrol car roll up and were already on their way back toward the street. The two patrolmen decided to split up their work—Joe would work his way along the back doors of the complex while Pat checked the front.

Cyrus had the two under his own surveillance and saw the opportunity to move in on Joe as they split up. Easing his car around toward the back of the complex from a neighboring parking lot, he parked and hunkered down. He could see Joe trying the doors, making sure they were locked. Cyrus had to move quickly, before Pat made it around to the back. He crept up on Joe, gun drawn, until he was less than six feet away.

"Don't say a word, you bastard. Turn around."

Joe slowly turned to face Kathleen's killer. "So it's you coming for me now. Problem is, Cyrus, I don't work alone."

Cyrus's eyes grew bigger, and he glanced over his

shoulder but saw no one. "Shut up. I hear poor Kathleen's lonely; thought I'd do something about it. Tell her I said hello."

Cyrus didn't hear Pat and Steve coming for him. He couldn't understand what strange force had thrown him to the ground and knocked the gun from his hand. But Cyrus fought. He wrestled the men trying to hold him down, tried to bite and kick them. Only when the burning mist of pepper spray shot fire into his eyes and nose did Cyrus give up. He was cuffed before he took his third breath and standing up in front of Joe before his fourth.

"See, Cyrus, the mistake Kathleen made was that she didn't come ready with backup. And I'm sure she never expected that her own family would try to hurt her. But I expected you, and I saw you. I saw you at my apartment complex, I saw you when I was running, and Pat saw you in the alleyway. You thought you were waiting for me, but we were waiting for you."

Cyrus stood mute in front of them all.

"Why'd you kill her, you son of a bitch?" Joe was beginning to lose his self-control.

"You'll never know…You'll never know."

Those were the last words Cyrus ever spoke to Joe again. Joe thought he would find closure in catching Cyrus, and in a way, he did. He could rest easier knowing the man would be put away for a very long time. But not understanding why was harder. He saw it every day on the job—people making foolish, sometimes dangerous choices—and he never really tried to figure out why. But now it was more personal, and it was difficult for him.

After Steve put Cyrus in his car for transport, Joe had Wendy call the chief. Joe made the chief aware that he believed Cyrus was on the prowl, and they had taken extra precautions in recent days. Joe had been tailed by an off-duty cop, who, by virtue of his presence, was following Cyrus as well. The chief was both thrilled and relieved at the arrest. He was worried sick that he might lose another officer, but Joe had played his cards right, letting in the people who would look out for him. The chief promised to call the Whitcomb County sheriff and Kathleen's parents. It had been a good night.

By the time he got off duty, Joe was exhausted. He promised to take Pat and Steve out for a beer or two once they got off, but both could tell from Joe's face that he needed rest more than alcohol. They begged off, promising to get together over the weekend. Joe was grateful, and he told them so.

Once home, Joe stood under the shower's stream until all the hot water washed down the drain. Outside the bathroom, the blast of refrigerated air made him a little light-headed, so he walked toward his bedroom to lie down. He stumbled in the doorway but caught himself on the chest of drawers. Looking down, he noticed that part of the wood on the front of the chest had given way, but the cut was smooth. He pulled on it and discovered Kathleen's stash of money.

"Well, damn, Kathleen, you *are* full of secrets."

It occurred to him that there may be other such compartments behind the decorative trim along the front and side of the piece. Joe gently pulled on each corner and facet, revealing another deep niche. Inside he unearthed notes, handwritten by Kathleen. Puzzled, Joe sat on his bed, a towel sarong wrapped around his waist, and began to read her words: "I can't decide just how much the town has changed over the years..." Joe felt neither sadness nor anger. But when he read about the two church steeples, one unpainted and one not, he noticed himself in the mirror, seated next to the memory of Kathleen, and knew that he was not alone.

## About the Author

Susan Anderson grew up a privileged Southern belle. She travelled overseas with her family, attended private schools, and debuted internationally. But that's not the life she chose for herself. Susan, like her grandfather, wanted to work in law enforcement. As a small-town cop, Susan found unique joy in helping and protecting her community, but her other passion, writing, drew her back to school for more studies. *Cold Case in Ellyson* is that intersection of her work as a cop colliding with her need to write.

Susan lives in Gulf Breeze, Florida with her husband and two sons. She shares tennis there with her friends, baseball with her boys, and good wine with her husband.

## From the Author

Although some of the names and locations in this book exist, *Cold Case in Ellyson* is a fictional piece of work. Some descriptions, particularly those on the job, may be based on actual events although she has taken liberties with them for the advancement of the book.

Made in the USA
Charleston, SC
02 July 2010